FIGHT FIRE WITH FIRE

FIGHT FIRE WITH FIRE

THE UNBELIEVABLE MR. BROWNSTONE BOOK SEVEN

MICHAEL ANDERLE

LMBPN

DISRUPTIVE IMAGINATION

FIGHT FIRE WITH FIRE TEAM

Special Thanks
to Mike Ross
for BBQ Consulting
Jessie Rae's BBQ - Las Vegas, NV

Thanks to the JIT Readers

John Ashmore
James Caplan
Mary Morris
Tim Bischoff
Peter Manis
Daniel Weigert
Paul Westman
Larry Omans
Micky Cocker

If I've missed anyone, please let me know!

Editor
Lynne Stiegler

*To Family, Friends and
Those Who Love
to Read.
May We All Enjoy Grace
to Live the Life We Are
Called.*

James' phone chimed. He rolled over in bed to check it when Shay grabbed his arm.

"Don't," she commanded.

He arched a brow. "Don't? What if it's important?"

"Leave it. It's a text, and I guarantee it's not important. If some giant zombie was rampaging through downtown and they needed your help they would call, not text you."

"But I'm already up. It doesn't hurt to check."

Shay laughed. "We're both up, so we should have some fun instead. Even if I can't walk straight after three days. Might as well chance not being able to move at all." She grinned. "I'm more than willing to take the risk."

James grunted. "Not complaining, but we can't relax forever."

"So boring." The tomb raider rolled her eyes. "I can't believe that a man who is an alien with a super-amulet can be this boring at times."

James shrugged and grabbed the phone. It wasn't a

message about some rampaging level-five bounty or a giant zombie, but it was from an important employee, Trey.

Yo, James. You ignoring me now? 'Sup with that? Other than that 'Yeah, I'm alive' shit you sent yesterday, you haven't sent crap back. Is this because I said I needed a favor? That ain't like you.

James texted back immediately.

Sorry. Just was distracted. If you need a favor, that's not a big deal. Last time you needed a favor, I got some nice bounty money out of it and took down a nasty son of a bitch. Any money in this one?

Trey's reply shot back a few seconds later.

I don't need a favor anymore, but Nana just called me and she needs one. She says she wants to talk to you about some shit ASAP. Doubt there's a lot of money in it. Nana's tough, but she ain't rich.

Okay. I'll be by soon. Don't want to piss her off and face her cane.

LOL. Yeah, right. Okay, thanks, James. I'll talk to you later.

James sighed. "I've got some things I need to take care of."

Shay sat up and laughed. "You know, the world won't end if you take a week off."

"It doesn't have to end. It just has to get shittier."

She groaned. "Is that what you've managed to do? Mindfuck yourself into believing that? It wasn't all that long ago that the only thing you cared about was if someone had a bounty, and now you're turning criminals into bounty hunters and adopting girls. You go for *barbeque* and you end up taking a guy down. I mean, shit, you probably pick up trash from the highway when I'm not around."

James grunted. "I got a bounty for that douchebag in Las Vegas."

Shay shook her head. "The point is, you were supposed to be there for *barbeque*, not work. Besides, isn't that what the Brownstone Agency is about? Taking some of the load off your shoulders?"

"Yeah, but some loads are too heavy for others to carry." He frowned.

"You're a good man, James. Probably too good for me." Shay gave him a sly wink.

James grunted and looked away. "Never too good for you. You're too good for me."

He threw the covers off and stood. As much as he'd like to dive back under the sheets for another day of sweaty exercise with Shay, if Trey's grandmother needed a favor he had to help. If it were something the rookie bounty hunter could handle by himself, he wouldn't have bothered James.

Shay hopped out of bed and sashayed naked toward the bathroom. "I never know when I might be heading out. I could be gone for a day or two weeks. Or I could get stuck in the Bermuda Triangle for a year. You sure?"

The bounty hunter grunted. "No, not sure, but guess I'll just have to suck it up and hope you don't get stuck in the Bermuda Triangle."

"Remember, most of those saints you admire so much died grizzly deaths." Shay pulled her toothbrush out of her crystal skull holder and started brushing her teeth. "Just sayin,'" she mumbled.

"We all end up dead. Only thing that matters is what we do in-between." James shrugged and grabbed a shirt, pants, and belt from his closet.

He allowed himself a small smile as he watched Shay brush her teeth. She was right about how he used to be, but he had changed. Life meant something now that he had someone to share it with, and a daughter to protect.

Shay didn't speak again until she'd finished brushing her teeth aggressively. No wonder they were so white. She slipped her toothbrush back into its holder just as James came into the bathroom to brush his teeth.

"You're not pissed, are you?"

Shay gave him a little bump with her hip and snickered. "Nope. I can't help it if I'm a Brownstone junkie. It's a good thing that you're forcing me to stop. If I spend too much more time with you, I might end up too sore to do my next job. You're saving me from myself. My hero." She offered him a seductive smile. "Still…how about at least joining me for a little shower? I need a little help getting soaped up. And you—you smell."

James lifted an arm and sniffed. "Would you look at that, I *do* smell." He grinned. "Wouldn't want to smell all day."

"That would be terrible." Shay winked and crooked her finger as she stepped into the shower.

***

Queen Laena stared out the window at the waves crashing on the beach below. Earth might be a primitive planet filled with murderous barbarians, but it did have its charms. Not that she wanted to ever live there. She didn't care what strange rumors swirled about the fate of Oriceran. She refused to abandon her world until it was less than a cinder.

Nothing but cowards and weakness on a planet filled with magic. Our people will not flee to Earth to beg for scraps from the humans. We are strong.

She'd visited Earth so many times as of late, but each time she'd failed to return to Oriceran with what her people truly needed if they were going to have a future.

The queen folded her hands behind her back as she continued to look outside. "Tell me you have something useful. I dislike having to stay on Earth longer than necessary." She sniffed disdainfully.

Three Drow stood behind Laena, three of her most loyal and competent servants. Widowmaker had also been one of her trusted servants, yet Widowmaker had failed her. It was fortunate that the human authorities hadn't thought to probe deeper into the body using magic.

The leader of the three, Zavan, cleared his throat. "Every time we try to trace the princess something blocks us. We suspect multiple spells. Powerful magic."

"More powerful than the Drow?"

Zavan lowered his eyes. "In this case, yes, my Queen."

Laena let out a labored sigh. Ignoring a strong foe wouldn't accomplish anything but the loss of more Drow. "Then whoever has her knows of her potential," she concluded. "But I would know if they'd already used the wish, so they are waiting, for some reason."

Zavan frowned. "What possible reason?"

The queen lifted her chin. "It doesn't matter. They have

stolen the legacy of our people. I don't care if they are Earthlings or Oricerans; they will be made to pay with their lives." The queen shook her head. "These locals and their Oriceran enablers have made things unnecessarily difficult. I can't stay and personally manage the search. I have duties." She narrowed her eyes. "As does the Princess of the Shadow Forged."

"Of course, my Queen," Zavan ceded. "Widowmaker had her talents, but her appetites easily distracted her. That won't be a problem for us."

Laena spun and marched toward the door. "Locate the princess. Don't cause too much trouble until then, but once you find her, I don't care what you have to do as long as you return her to Oriceran. Once I have her there, I'll have fewer restrictions on what I can do to ensure the power of our people."

She threw open the door and stalked out of the room with her head held high.

Zavan winced as his queen slammed the door. He glanced at his partners, Kaella and Reyal. The two Drow women were powerful, intelligent, and focused, unlike Widowmaker. His group wouldn't fail.

"We need to locate the girl before the queen decides we're incompetent."

Kaella crossed her arms. "Obviously. But our scrying magic keeps failing, and we don't understand this *Los Angeles* well enough to know who to talk to. The damned Light Elves have infested this area, and they are watching us."

Reyal, the shorter of the two woman, snorted. "We shouldn't go begging for help from others. We should maintain our pride." She took a deep breath and slowly let it out, her brow furrowed in anger. "The previous princess shamed her people." Her lip curled. "To take up with a *human*? Pathetic. I only regret she didn't live long enough to be punished by the queen."

"It doesn't matter," Zavan replied. "Once we recover the current princess, the queen will make her understand she is a Drow and not a human. She can't be blamed for the deceptions of her mother."

"James Brownstone," Kaella announced. "He's still our best lead. We also know he's not as dangerous as everyone claims. *One* of us could kill the man, let alone three of us."

Zavan arched a brow. "Why do you say that? Have you heard something?"

"He didn't kill Widowmaker. The humans did." She sneered. "From what they've said, they were told that she would be there. It was a trap."

"So?"

Kaella flung her arms up. "So this means James Brownstone is a coward, afraid to face a Drow in direct battle."

Reyal shook her head. "But he wouldn't have even known she was a Drow—or that she was hunting him."

Kaella refused to be swayed. "Who else then? He was her target. Somehow he figured it out and ran from battle. It means he's too afraid to face a powerful foe in battle."

Zavan rubbed his chin. "Perhaps, but we can't be so sure. If he was the one who trapped Widowmaker, it would mean he's smarter than we've heard."

The three exchanged a glance and burst out laughing.

Zavan calmed down, his laughter subsiding into a few lingering chuckles. "No. He got lucky, or he has some powerful friends. We will continue to focus on him, and we will make him lead us to the princess, wherever he's hiding her."

"And what if he resists us?"

His pleasant smile disappeared, replaced by a vicious grin. "Then he will experience the true wrath of the Drow."

Maria stepped out of her car and hoisted her laden backpack onto her shoulder. Her mood was dark as she made her way to the rusty metal stairs leading to the second floor of the apartment building. She marched toward Dannec's place, wondering if the door would even be there this time. With the elf's magic, she could never be sure.

Why does magic have to be so damn annoying?

Not only was the door there, but it opened as she stepped up to it. Dannec stood on the other side with an amused look on his face.

Okay, at least that's not annoying.

"Good afternoon, Lieutenant."

The AET officer's head jerked from side to side. "Don't use my title out here," she barked.

Dannec dismissed her concerns with a wave. "Don't worry. That you're coming to my place signals the kind of person you are to anyone who lives here."

She frowned, not sure she liked the implications of that. "So? A lot of people might enjoy taking out a cop. A lot of magical people might particularly like to take out an AET officer."

"Perhaps, but none would be so unwise to attempt that

when you're my guest." Dannec gestured inside. "Please come in."

Maria stepped inside the apartment, eyeing the tables covered with artifacts as she followed Dannec. The extra-dimensional chest was either absent or hidden with magic; she couldn't be sure.

"First of all," she began, "let me thank you for your help. Without the deflectors you provided, we would have suffered some serious injuries. That murderer we took down was a psychotic bitch."

Dannec made a face. "I watched part of the video on the internet. She was using dark and infernal magic. It's a good thing you killed her before she hurt other people. Her kind burn out quickly, but they are capable of great harm."

"'Burn out?'"

Dannec nodded. "Magic isn't so different from human science, Lieutenant. Everything has a cost; a price. It uses a person as much as they use it. Killing blindly for the sake of killing is dangerous to the person doing it." He shrugged. "Maybe she was doing it as a sacrifice to the creatures she used, but from what I read about the slaughter before your confrontation, she appeared to just enjoy killing." He sneered. "Even Rhazdon rarely killed without a purpose."

Maria didn't know much about the Atlantean version of Hitler, but she got the point. "I'm working on the payment. Tyler's finishing setting up his business so I can pay through it."

"You mean funnel money through it." Dannec chuckled.

Maria's neck tensed and her stomach tightened. She'd pushed a lot of the implications of her work with Dannec out of her mind, especially given the results. However, the elf was right. She might have saved cop and civilian lives, but she was so over the line at this point that she might as well be in Alaska.

Doesn't matter. Eventually, I might go down, but in the meantime, I don't care. Not if it means I can protect cops and save people from overpowered magical assholes who want to slaughter them in the streets.

Maria squared her shoulders and tilted her chin up. "The point is that I can push a *lot* of money through Tyler."

"I'm satisfied with how things are progressing, and I don't feel any guilt, Lieutenant. Whatever you might believe about me and where I get my items, the fact is all I've done with you so far is help you stop a monster."

Maria chuckled darkly. "And I'm sure Robert Johnson figured all he'd done was acquire really great guitar-playing skills."

Dannec furrowed his brow. "Who?"

"He's a famous American musician. Legend says he sold his soul to the Devil at a crossroads for guitar-playing skill."

The elf laughed. "How wasteful. There are plenty of spells for musical prowess that don't require you to sell your soul. Foolish human."

Maria opened her mouth to explain that it was only a story, but closed it and shrugged. Given what she did on a daily basis, she couldn't say the legend wasn't true. While she highly doubted the bluesman had sold his soul to the literal *Devil*, she wouldn't put it past some Oriceran asshole to have popped over to Mississippi to collect a free soul in exchange for what Dannec implied wasn't even that powerful a kind of magic.

"Problem, Lieutenant?" Dannec inquired.

"Nothing, just got a little lost in thought." Maria slid the backpack off her shoulder. "Got some deflectors in here. Can you recharge the ones we used?"

Dannec inclined his head just a touch too slowly to hide the smile at the corner of his mouth. "I'd be more than happy to. It will, of course, cost."

Maria raised her eyebrow. "Of course. Money, I hope, and not more favors."

"I need money more at the moment than favors, so yes."

She handed over the backpack. "How much?"

Dannec took a quick look inside the backpack. "I'll have to examine them first to see how much effort it'll take, but I can assure you, it'll be *much* cheaper than new deflectors."

Maria sighed. "Okay, just let Tyler know, and he'll pass it along to me. The less trail I leave for this stuff, the better."

Dannec gave her a broad smile, his eyes twinkling with merriment. "As always, a pleasure doing business with you."

Maria wondered if the Devil offered lower prices.

2

James hopped out of his F-350 in front of Trey's grandmother's house, wondering if he should have pressed his friend more on what sort of favor she wanted. She was aware of his reputation as a bounty hunter, so he assumed it involved kicking somebody's ass. However, if it was just a simple bounty, why hadn't she asked her grandson to handle it?

It wasn't like the old lady frequented criminal hangouts, so she shouldn't have had any run-ins with level-three or higher bounties.

Maybe she just has some nasty animals in her yard she wants me to scare off. Whatever it is should be easy shit to handle.

James grunted as he walked up the brick path to her front door. The kids and parents in Las Vegas wouldn't have expected to have to deal with a level-four bounty either. Douchebags drunk on power didn't stick to ratholes and caves. If they did, James wouldn't have a job.

If some magical douchebag is messing with an old woman, he's gonna be very fucking sorry. And very hurt, soon.

The bounty hunter knocked on the door, continuing to conjure up weird-ass scenarios such as the possibility that Trey's grandmother had run into a necromancer while buying groceries.

Fucking necromancers. Why don't you just let a woman buy her toilet paper and pork in peace, you sonsabitches?

Charlyce, Trey's aunt, and now an administrative assistant for the Brownstone Agency, opened the door and put a finger to her mouth.

"You're nothing but a little fool," Trey's grandmother yelled from the living room. "I can't believe you're such a fool that you'd come here and spew this garbage to my face in my home."

What the hell? Did Trey piss her off? Did he call him over here to save his ass from his grandmother?

James frowned. He didn't want to get in the middle of a family fight.

Charlyce opened the door wider. It wasn't Trey standing there, but one of his boys. The bounty hunter was moving away from calling them gang members now that they'd left the streets to train as new bounty hunters and information gatherers for the Brownstone Agency, but they'd always be Trey's boys in his mind.

"Garbage?" the former gang member shouted. "It ain't nothing but the truth. Fuck Brownstone, that bitch."

Guess I'm in the middle of this, but at least it's not a family matter.

James recognized the angry young man as nineteen-year-old Lachlan. From what Trey had told him, the kid was having more trouble adjusting to life off the street than a lot of the others. He'd given up on the gang, dissatisfied with the direction Trey was taking things.

That had left Lachlan with nowhere to go, since no other gangs had dared try to move into the neighborhood. Word had gotten out, not only about how Trey's gang were now the arms of James Brownstone, but also about when the Demon Generals had torn up the neighborhood and both the cops and Brownstone had beat them down.

An individual gang might be willing to risk a confrontation with the cops, Trey's boys, or Brownstone, but not all three. The territory just wasn't worth the hassle.

James hadn't cared about Lachlan leaving, but now he was causing trouble. That made it his problem again.

You should have just stayed away, kid, and not fucked with an old woman.

"Don't talk to me like that, boy," Trey's grandmother shouted, brandishing her cane at Lachlan.

The gang member snorted. "I didn't come here for your permission, old lady. I came here to let you know that your grandson had better watch it. This neighborhood needs a gang leader, and if he's given up, I'm gonna take that position. If that bitch Trey gets in my way, I'll beat his ass down." He smacked his fist into his palm. "I'ma beat *anyone's* ass down who gets in my way."

The old woman laughed in Lachlan's face. "Listen to you. Nothing but nonsense. First of all, boy, Trey hasn't given up anything. He decided to become someone worthy of respect, and he made sure to bring you all along, but you —you're gonna throw that away? Fool. You're a little boy pretending to be a man. It's pathetic."

"I don't want no fucking respect." Lachlan snarled. "I want people to be *afraid* of me."

"Don't matter. You want to run the gang that controls the neighborhood?"

"That's damned right. I'm gonna be the new shit around here, and everyone's gonna know not to fuck with this neighborhood."

I can't take this bullshit much longer.

Charlyce shook her head as she stepped aside to let James enter. The bounty hunter's fingers itched to toss this little asshole onto the lawn for the way he was disrespecting Trey's grandmother, but he refrained. The woman would ask for help if she needed it.

Besides, he'd seen her cane-wielding skills in action. She had this.

Trey's grandmother shook her head. "You can't run the gang, boy. This neighborhood already has a gang, and there's no way you have a chance against the man running the gang."

Lachlan scoffed. "Trey? Fuck that bitch. He ain't so tough."

The old woman pointed her cane at him. "This is your last warning, boy, and I'm not talking about Trey. I'm talking about James Brownstone. Trey works for him. *All* the boys work for him, which means he runs the gang now." She laughed. "You think you can take on James Brownstone? You think you can take on the Granite Ghost? HA! You'd have to be high to believe that."

"Brownstone's nothin' but a bitch who keeps getting lucky. I only di'n't pop his sorry ass because he's up to his neck with the 5-0 and I don't need *them* breathing down my neck. I wouldn't even need my gun. He'd be crying on his knees, begging me to leave him alone. Don't matter how tough he is. He ain't bulletproof."

James smiled at himself. *Not all the time. But some of the time.*

Charlyce rolled her eyes, and James grunted quietly and shook his head. Seeing wasn't believing for dumbasses. The Harriken had proven that, and he'd been forced to destroy them.

He'd heard enough of this crap. The old lady could defend her own honor, but Lachlan needed to be put in his place before he went and spread this bullshit attitude to the other former gang members. It was time to use a little phrase that Staff Sergeant Royce seemed fond of.

"Lachlan," James rumbled. "We need to have a little talk, and it's gonna be one way."

Lachlan flew through the air, flailing his arms until he smashed into the front yard with a grunt and rolled several feet.

Guess that was more of a demonstration than a talk.

James stuck the man's gun in his waistband as he stepped through the front door. "For a guy who didn't need his gun, you sure went for it fast, asshole."

The younger man groaned. "Fuck you, Brownstone."

"Good, you've still got some backbone. That means Royce can turn you into something other than a piece of shit who yells at old ladies." James marched over to the downed man and grabbed him by the neck. "So I'm gonna give you the opportunity to be something else."

James stomped over to the F-350, Lachlan in hand. He threw open the back door and tossed the dazed wannabe gang kingpin in the back.

Lachlan moaned.

The bounty hunter chuckled. "Don't complain. I'm still a lot nicer than Royce."

Shay swiped through the messages on her phone. Peyton had lined up some potential jobs, and if James didn't want to keep playing doctor, it was as good a time as any for her to go find out about the latest insane artifact someone wanted her to collect.

Someday I'm gonna have to tell James the truth about all the alien shit I know, but after that speech earlier there's no way. Need to protect him from himself.

Shay's phone rang and she answered, seeing that the call was from James.

"Regret leaving me already?" Shay purred. "You can always come back and correct the mistake. I'm still in town...for now."

James grunted. "I'd much rather be at my house doing shit with you than playing truant officer with some punk kid with delusions of grandeur so bad that he makes King Pyro look humble."

All of Shay's passion drained from her. *"Truant officer?* What are you talking about?"

"One of the boys who quit Trey's gang was harassing

his Nana, going on about how he was gonna kick my ass and take over the gang and be the badass of the neighborhood. Shit like that."

Shay laughed. "I'm guessing that ended *real* well for him. Don't these dumbasses ever learn?"

James grunted. "He's just a punk kid so I didn't send him through a wall, even though I was tempted. Plus, it'd be a dick move against Trey's grandmother since I was in her house."

"But I'm guessing there was still some violence involved?"

"I just helped him move from one point to another real fast."

Shay snickered. "And what happened after that?"

"I've got him in my truck now, and I'm taking him to the Brownstone Building for a little 'Marine re-education.'"

"The fun's definitely over then." She sighed. "No way in hell you're coming back this morning, is there?"

"Sorry," James rumbled. "But I'll make it up to you. How about we have a date night before you head out again? You said you weren't leaving right away."

She resisted the urge to tell him that she might end up getting a job that required just that. The last thing she wanted to do was guilt-trip the man and get clingy.

Shay pondered the original offer. "Sure, but this time I don't want to go anywhere fancy."

"You don't?" James chuckled. "Fine by me. You're the one who is obsessed with us going to fancy places. It's not like I love having to go to a place that requires different types of forks. Why the change?"

"It's hard to get blood out of a lot of fabrics, and I want

to make sure if any assholes show up, I'm able to join in the fun and not just leave you to have all of it."

"Okay, I'll think of something. One sec." She could hear James speaking over the phone, but his voice was distant and muffled. Scratching filled the line before he came back. "Sorry, just needed to explain some shit to Lachlan. I'll think of someplace appropriate for our date. Talk to you later."

"Talk to you later."

James ended the call.

Shay sighed and surveyed the disaster that was the bedroom. Her clothes were strewn all around the floor, and the sheets were more than a little used after their epic three-day romp. They'd barely left the room other than to eat.

She was surprised James hadn't freaked out more about the mess, but she'd done a damned good job of distracting him with her body. Now that the pleasure marathon was over, OCD James was sure to return.

Shay gathered her clothes from the floor. If she cleaned up and washed the sheets, it'd elevate James' mood after he finished smacking around his employee. It was the little things.

Managing with only Peyton is easy. I got all the death threats out of the way early on. Then again, James doesn't have to deal with shit like that gnome, so maybe we're even.

The tomb raider leaned over and hissed at an ache shooting through her body. The days of fun had taken a toll on her. She wasn't usually this sore unless she got in a fight or fell from a mountain. It also pissed her off that

James was feeling well enough to go manhandle some gang member.

"That asshole is still walking around like he's some sort of Superman..." Shay gasped. "Shit. I didn't think about it before."

Like Superman, James was an alien from another planet, most likely sent by his parents. Also, like Superman, James was stronger than the average human, even without his amulet. Finally like Superman, James had been raised by good people with a strong moral center and had internalized the desire to fight evil, even if he'd tried to hide it behind bullshit defenses about being nothing more than a bounty hunter.

Shay snickered. It was a good thing James hadn't ended up being adopted by her parents. If so, New York would have been a burnt-out crater already.

"Wait. If he's Superman, that means I'm *fucking* Superman! Who does that make me, Lois Lane?"

The tomb raider snorted and grabbed her bra off the ground.

3

Trey stared at the huge mud pit and shook his head. Even though he'd been told about it before, he still wasn't crazy about the idea. Fighting a group of men didn't bother him, but rolling around in the mud just didn't appeal.

Every day when he got up he slapped on a suit like he was going to an office—only *his* office was the streets of Los Angeles. The suit projected respectability and filled him with confidence. The idea of rolling around in the mud like some drunken pig only filled him with the urge to rebel.

Shit. I'm gonna have to set an example for my boys. No way to get out of this bullshit.

"Listen up, men," Staff Sergeant Royce shouted.

"Yes, Staff Sergeant," the assembled trainees yelled in unison.

Trey, James, and Chris Royce had discussed whether to make use of his old rank when he started training the gang members. They concluded that it'd help reinforce discipline during the training process.

The ex-gangbangers didn't respect *most* authority figures, but almost to a man they respected the military—and the Marine Corps in particular. He wouldn't wear his uniform because he was retired, but the title still carried weight with them.

"You've come a long way from the lazy-ass undisciplined pieces of shit you were when I started with you," the drill instructor continued. "But you've still got a long fucking way to go. It is fortunate that I don't have to turn your weak asses into Marines, just bounty hunters, so there's some tiny hope for you yet." He pointed to the pit. "Part of not being a puppy pretending to be a man is commanding respect in difficult environments. At the end of the week, we're going to find out who is the King of the Pit. Everyone's going to get involved on two teams."

Trey was distracted by a movement off to the side. A foul-faced Lachlan marched out of the back of the Brownstone Building, the big man himself behind him. James looked more bored than annoyed.

Lachlan had left the gang recently, and Trey wasn't surprised to see he'd run into trouble with James. He'd expected to have to confront the asshole sooner or later.

A sudden thought had the former gang leader grimacing. "Shit, James," Trey began. "Please tell me that this stupid motherfucker wasn't at Nana's house. Please tell me he was just walking down the street and flipped your ass off or something."

The gathered men laughed.

James pushed Lachlan forward. "He was having an

argument with your grandmother. I had to remove him for his own safety before she beat his ass *down.*"

Lachlan scoffed. "I don't need no protection from some old bi—"

James spun Lachlan around and glared at him. "Don't make the mistake of thinking that me making a few jokes means I'm gonna stand here and let you disrespect that woman. You understand me, asshole?"

Lachlan glared back. "Fuck you, Brownstone."

Royce stepped forward with a deep scowl on his face, more than ready to go all *Full Metal Jacket* on the wayward gang member.

Trey shook his head and held up a hand. Lachlan was younger and had always been trouble. Trey led the gang, so the gang members—former or current—were his responsibility.

He waved Royce down. "I got this," he told him, meeting Lachlan's eyes as he marched toward him.

James grunted and shoved the man toward his former gang leader.

Trey loomed over Lachlan. "You think you got something to prove, bitch?"

Lachlan sneered. "No. I think *you* do. You fucking gave up. You're nothing but Brownstone's bitch, so I'm taking over the gang. Once I do, everyone in his neighborhood will know who the real bitch is."

Everyone laughed, except for James and Royce.

"Yeah, 'Lachlan, King of the Streets,'" a man jeered. "Fuck it, why not King of Los Angeles? Next thing you know, it'll be like, 'Oh shit, Mr. President, I'm sorry, sir.'"

"Maybe he should start a new Harriken," another man called. "Then Brownstone can kill *their* asses, too."

Trey held up his hand, and everyone quieted down. "You're gonna lead the gang, Lachlan? No one's gonna follow you, bitch. A fucking stray dog you gave a steak to wouldn't follow you. You've never been the brightest guy, but now you're just being a dumbass."

Lachlan seethed with rage. "You think you're so tough, Trey. Fuck you."

"I don't *think* I'm tough. I *know* I'm tough." Trey laughed. "Fuck, I don't even need to prove it. I've got an official list of bounty captures that anyone can look at on the net. What you got, Lachlan? Big words? Look at you! You're just a kid. I know you think you've got something to prove. That you are the baddest motherfucker around, or some stupid shit like that. But my patience only goes so fucking far, *especially* when you involve my nana."

Lachlan puffed up his chest. "*I* am the baddest mother-fucker, and I don't want to work with no pussies."

"You think Staff Sergeant Royce is a *pussy?*" Trey glowered at Lachlan. "He was fighting terrorists and weird-ass monsters when you were still wetting your bed, bitch." He pointed at James. "And Mr. Brownstone is such a badass he don't even have time to beat low-level bitches like you down no more." He waved toward the men. "This is why we're here. Know your place. You want to be a tough guy? Fucking *prove* it."

"Whatever. I don't even fucking care about any of you bitches. I only care about me."

"Fine." Trey squared his shoulders. "But you *should* care, and if you want to have a real future, then you need to understand that Mr. Brownstone is your boss now. No, fuck that. Mr. Brownstone is your *leader*. Maybe I should knock that shit into your head so you understand, motherfucker."

The men all hooted and hollered. Everyone wanted to see Trey lay out Lachlan. It'd be easy enough to do, but the man needed to be humbled even more, and Trey had an idea on how to go about accomplishing that.

"You think you're tough, Lachlan?"

"I fucking *know* it, Trey."

"Then let me show you what being part of Brownstone's Agency is all about," Trey declared. "Shorty, get your ass out here."

A broad-shouldered man a good head shorter than Lachlan stepped out of the crowd, cracking his knuckles.

Trey nodded to him. "You see, Shorty only came in a month ago. His mouth is three times the size of his dick, but he don't have the bad attitude you have, Lachlan. He's learned fucking respect for me, Mr. Brownstone, and Staff Sergeant Royce. How is it that a man who's only been with us for a month has respect, but your bitch ass never managed to?"

"He ain't *shit*," Lachlan declared. "You ain't shit." He pointed at Royce. "And I don't need G.I. Joe over there to make me into a badass. I'ma take all you fucking bitches down one by one if I have to."

Trey shook his head a little sadly. *Fuuuck, this bitch is stupid. I almost feel bad for what's about to happen to him.*

Royce snorted. The crowd laughed. James continued to watch impassively, understanding the importance of Trey working through the dynamics of his gang.

Trey snorted. "Shorty ain't shit? Staff Sergeant Royce ain't shit? You see, here's the thing. You've *got* no gang, bitch. *I* had a gang, and now Brownstone has a group of employees who *used* to be in the gang. *That's* what's up. If you don't like it, you've got one of two choices. You can walk away and don't fuck with us, or join us and learn how to become a real man, not some whiny bitch."

"Fuck you. You ain't my leader anymore. I don't have to listen to you."

"Yeah, you're right. I ain't your leader. So this is just about proving who really is a badass. Shorty's gotten real training. He has discipline. He ain't a Marine, but he's been trained by one. He can take your ass down for sure."

Lachlan gave Trey a feral grin. "Fine. I bet your ass that I can take out that bitch Shorty without breaking a sweat." He shrugged. "You love playing Marine so much? Then all you fuckers can do two hundred push-ups while I laugh at your asses. I'm gonna go around the neighborhood talking about how weak-ass you bitches are."

Trey nodded. "Fine, but if Shorty takes *your* ass out, you'd better join back up and stop your bitching."

"Whatever. Sure. It ain't gonna happen."

Trey stepped back. Shorty advanced, a smirk on his face.

"Don't beat him too bad, Shorty. I want him to be able to train without having to go the hospital first."

The other men started cheering Shorty on.

"Better get ready to do your push-ups, Trey." Lachlan shook out his hands and raised his fists. "Come on, Shorty. I bet your dick is as short as you are."

The other man advanced, still smirking. "You know what your problem is, asshole?"

"What?"

"You don't read enough. Staff Sergeant has us doing a lot of reading. Lots of good shit like Marcus Aurelius and Sun Tzu. You need to read *Art of War*, bitch."

Lachlan scoffed. "What? What the fuck is that?"

"Sun Tzu was an ancient Chinese strategy badass who studied war and wrote all the good shit down. Staff Sergeant always tells us that being disciplined isn't just about the body, it's about the mind." Shorty pointed to his head. "That's your problem, bitch. You don't have a disciplined body *or* mind."

Lachlan laughed. "That's what these bitches have you doing? Reading? *That's* making you into badasses? What-the-fuck-ever."

"Sun Tzu says that if you know yourself and you know your enemy, then you'll have a hundred battles with a hundred victories."

"What the fuck does that even mean? Might as well be speaking Chinese."

Shorty took a few steps forward. "Here's the thing. I know myself. Staff Sergeant Royce has made me a bitch at times, but he's shown me the kind of man I am. My limits." He pointed at Lachlan. "But you ran away, bitch. You don't know your limits. You don't know mine. You're all noise; barking. Fuck, Marcus Aurelius knew all that shit, too, and he was a motherfucking emperor. He said, 'You have power over your mind, not outside events. Realize this, and you will find strength.'" He shook his head. "You don't know yourself, and you don't have power over your mind. You've already lost."

Lachlan shrugged and snorted. "What the fuck? I thought this Marine was supposed to be turning you all into badasses, but now you're running around quoting dead fucks like it means shit. I'm gonna beat your ass down, then you can tell me what motherfucking Marcus Aurelius and Sun Tzu have to say about *that* shit."

He took a wide swing. Shorty grabbed his arm and spun in one fluid motion, taking advantage of the other man's momentum to send him flying to the ground.

The crowd erupted into laughter.

Shorty grinned. "Sun Tzu would probably say, 'Victorious warriors win first and then go to war, while defeated warriors go to war first and then seek to win.'"

"Fuck Sun Tzu." Lachlan pushed off the ground. "You got lucky, bitch. You think some moldy Chinese bitch is gonna help you win against me?"

"One battle, one victory." Shorty gestured for Lachlan to attack. "Ninety-nine more to go, bitch. I could do this all day."

Lachlan yelled and charged. Shorty sidestepped and slammed his elbow into the man's back. Lachlan collapsed to the ground with a grunt, grimacing in pain.

Shorty stepped back and shook his head. "See, if this was a *real* fight, I'd be stomping the shit out of your head right now. Or I would have pulled a gun and put a bullet into you." He slammed his foot once into the downed man's stomach. "Marcus Aurelius had some shit to say about being a good man. Guess I failed that test today."

"That's enough," Trey yelled.

Shorty snorted and headed back into the crowd.

"We ain't done," Lachlan wheezed.

"The fuck you ain't," Trey yelled. "It's like he said. He only didn't beat your ass into a coma because I didn't want him to. You've always been a dumbass, Lachlan." He motioned to the collected trainees. "You want to be tough? You want to be a part of the baddest motherfucking gang in Los Angeles? Then you join the Brownstone Agency. There ain't a single motherfucker in this country who is more badass than James Brownstone. He's proven it again and again and again to bigger and badder fuckers who only thought they were tough."

James grunted but didn't say anything else.

"Combat training, fitness, strategy, discipline," Trey rattled off. "*That's* the kind of shit Staff Sergeant Royce is filling the boys with. They ain't gangbangers anymore. They're trainee bounty hunters. Men who fucking think *before* they throw a punch. Men who understand shit like Sun Tzu and understand that the world may change, but some things stay the same. Attitude ain't everything."

Lachlan sat up and wiped some blood from the edge of his mouth. "You're okay with following Brownstone?"

Trey shook his head. "Do you not believe your mother-fucking eyes and ears, Lachlan? Mr. Brownstone could kill every last one of our asses by himself without breaking a sweat." He pointed at James, who shrugged. "He already took down an entire gang, not to mention all those magic freaks."

"I did have one person helping me some of the time with the Harriken," James clarified. "But I killed more people. I had to stop counting after a while so I can't give you exact numbers."

The men all laughed, and Trey smirked.

"If you want to be something other than a bitch, Lachlan, then join up. Staff Sergeant Royce will run your ass through the grinder, but at the end of the day, you'll be proud of yourself because you'll be a real man. Not this weak-ass excuse you are right now. If you're too much of a pussy to handle what it takes to be a member of the Brownstone Agency, then I don't give a fuck. You can walk away." Trey grabbed him by his shirt collar. "But this neighborhood belongs to the Brownstone Agency, and if you fuck with *anyone* in the agency or their families, we'll show you just what a little training has done for us. You fucking understand me?"

He released his grip, and the defeated gangbanger slumped.

"Okay," Lachlan murmured. "I... I guess I want in."

Detectives West and Lafayette of the Las Vegas Metropolitan Police Department sat in the break room with coffee and a few donuts on the table in front of them.

Lafayette looked at his partner who was scowling. "What? Coffee too strong again?"

West shook his head. "No. Just was thinking about the Red-Eyes Killer."

"Why? It's over. Brownstone took him out. That fucker has gone to explain himself to the Devil now."

"I'm glad he's gone, but I also can't stop thinking about

what would have happened if we hadn't had Brownstone here. The Feds may have carted off all those mutants they had in the lower levels of that lab, but Red Eyes only didn't get to them because of Brownstone. He had the contacts and the power to take the asshole down."

Lafayette took a bite of a maple bar and swallowed. "Isn't that the textbook definition of 'All's well that ends well?'"

"Maybe, but imagine if Brownstone hadn't been around. Red Eyes took out a level-four bounty hunter. If Brownstone hadn't shown up, he would have freed his freak buddies and it would have been a damned massacre. How many people would have died? Dozens? Hundreds? Thousands?" West shook his head. "Think about that shit in LA with that witch who went berserk at the farmer's market? We don't have the kind of AET resources they do. By the time reinforcements or the National Guard arrived, it'd be too late."

His partner shrugged. "More freaks like to hit LA than Vegas. I don't know if it's the Mafia or if we're sitting on top of some ancient dragon or some shit, but Red Eyes was the worst thing we've had to deal with since that few days where they were talking about moving Jessie Rae's to New York."

West shrugged. "That kind of muscle could help with other shit, too, though."

"Like that?"

"Mafia, for one. I mean we had them on the run with the help of the Feds, and then all this magic shit happens and they're stronger than ever." West slammed his fist on the table, almost spilling some coffee. "Those sonsabitches were behind Red Eyes. We need more resources. Manpower. People who can go places us cops can't."

Lafayette eyed his coffee and picked it up, afraid his partner was going to spill it during his next rant. "I agree, but without a clear high-end threat, it's not like we can request someone like Brownstone to show up."

"No, we can't, but maybe we don't have to." West nodded and looked down, his brow furrowed in his concentration.

"What are you talking about?"

"Brownstone's not just Brownstone anymore."

"Huh?"

"His agency. We don't have a bunch of level fours, fives, or sixes running around, but we do have lower-level bounties. We should look into getting his agency to help us. It'll also help get us in tighter with Brownstone should we need him."

"Huh. It wouldn't hurt to check with the captain."

4

Zavan settled on the leather couch. It was comfortable enough, even if the light color scheme favored in the rental house wasn't to his taste. They'd paid for three months with the help of a little gold converted to dollars, and they also had access to the human internet. He still didn't understand it all that well, but Kaella had no such problems, even without the use of the Skill Ring he'd had to give to Reyal.

The other Drow woman had been tasked with getting them a vehicle.

When they'd brought the Skill Ring over from Oriceran, Zavan had assumed they'd need it to use some sort of Earth weapon. It had never occurred to him that it might prove more useful for such a banal task as transportation. They could use magic to fly, teleport, or gate around with ease, but that'd only draw more attention. Blending in, or at least not standing out, would help them with their mission.

"Zavan, come here," Kaella called from the computer desk.

He stood and made his way over. An image of Brownstone's mottled face dominated the screen.

"I already know what he looks like," the Drow declared. "How is this useful?"

Kaella shook her head. "This site, YouTube, is a repository of human recordings. They have many of Brownstone."

Zavan nodded slowly. He grabbed a nearby chair and sat. "Let's see what we're truly up against, then."

Kaella moved the mouse and clicked on a video entitled *Brownstone Beats Down Bikers. Now With Added Soundtrack.*

The video began. Brownstone stood in a parking lot with six bikers surrounding him. They rushed him, but his punches sent them flying farther than a blow from a human should. Light classical music played in the background.

Zavan narrowed his eyes.

The short clip ended moments later with the bikers defeated.

"Magically-enhanced strength," he observed. "But defeating human riffraff is hardly impressive."

Kaella selected another video called *The King is dead! Long live the King!*

The shaky video appeared to have been taken from some distance up, perhaps from a human vehicle such as a helicopter.

A flaming man smashed through the window of a bank. A short battle followed in which the pyromancer blasted away at Brownstone, only to end with the bounty hunter pummeling the man's head into nothingness in a parking lot.

Zavan tilted his head. The defeat of the pyromancer was impressive, but he was more surprised by the large number of human police in the parking lot.

"Resistance to flame as well, it seems," he commented. "And he inspires enough terror or respect that the human authorities give him a wide berth and let him face down enemies."

"Look at this one. It's called *Brownstone Stops the Apocalypse in Mexico*."

Zavan snorted. "Humans are so easily impressed."

Again, the clip appeared to be from an aerial camera, but the quality of the image and the magnification were awful compared to the pyromancer battle.

In the video, a group of shambling humans surrounded a single man who was shooting, punching, and kicking them. It might have been Brownstone, but it was hard to tell given the poor quality and distance.

"The movement of these humans is odd," Kaella commented.

Zavan leaned forward. "Oh, I understand now. These are undead. Some necromancer, I assume." The video clip ended up abruptly. "What's wrong?"

Kaella shrugged. "That's all that was posted."

Another video followed: *LAPD Drone: Brownstone vs. Magical Russian Mobster (Attempt #5 View before the Man takes this down) Warning: Graphic content!!!!*

In the brief clip, Brownstone threw several punches at a larger man in a suit. Despite the bounty hunter's previously demonstrated strength, his blows didn't strike the man. Instead, a blue field winked into existence with each blow. The bounty hunter's enemy grabbed his arm and said something, but even if the drone had managed to record the words, the uploader had overlain some pounding human techno music that drowned out any other sound.

Zavan found himself beginning to wonder how Brownstone would even survive the encounter when the bounty hunter stabbed his enemy through the throat with a knife.

"I'm beginning to think we may have underestimated James Brownstone."

Kaella nodded her agreement.

The next few hours passed with them watching James Brownstone deliver beatdown after beatdown to a variety of enemies both magical and not, including him marching straight into the local Harriken headquarters after a rather explosive initial attack.

Not every battle the man had fought was available to view online, but various fan websites—including Scourge of Harriken, Granite Ghost Groupies, and Brownstone Beatdown Central—offered detailed descriptions of other encounters, including a telepathic monster in Japan, a soul-stealing assassin, and most recently, a twisted mutant in Las Vegas born of science and dark magic.

Kaella blinked as she finished reading a description of how the bounty hunter had decapitated the mutant to defeat its regenerative capabilities. "There are things we're missing."

"Such as?"

"Brownstone has walked through fire-blasts and gunfire unscathed. He has powerful defensive spells in addition to his strength. In one of those videos, something moved without him touching it."

"I don't care. We have powerful spells, too. Besides, all these victories can help us." Zavan chuckled. "This will work to our advantage."

"How so? It'll be a difficult battle even with the three of us, and we'll have to isolate him. According to the rumors on Scourge of Harriken, he might have received aid from someone almost as lethal as he is."

Zavan snorted. "Have some pride as a Drow." He pointed to a picture of Brownstone standing in a park in front of a grill. "This arrogant *barbeque* lover has won many victories, I'll grant him that. But now he has these worshippers. These fools giving him names like 'Scourge of Harriken.'"

"He *did* wipe them out," Kaella muttered.

"So? They were humans with little magic. How difficult could it have been? You or I could have done the same thing, but look at what we've seen. He was a powerful man before, but he did not receive such adulation until recently. This means something important. And we can use it."

Kaella looked up from the computer. "I don't understand. What does it mean?"

"It means he's allowing the praise. He's let his petty victories against weak foes go to his head. He's not prepared to face a true foe. More than ever, I believe he was afraid to face Widowmaker."

"You're sure of this?"

"Yes. He might be more powerful than I realized physically, but his spirit has become weak."

The Drow woman clicked on a hyperlink and a picture

of a smiling Light Elf, also standing in front of a grill, popped up. The Drow took a moment to read the article, and both scowled at the same time.

"This is what comes of mixing too much with the Earth humans," Zavan spat out. "This Nadina has lowered herself to cook with humans and seek their praise. The sooner we find the princess and leave this wretched place, the better."

James sat down at the desk in his office. He almost never used the place, so it contained only his desk, a couple of chairs, and a phone. But at least it gave him somewhere to talk with people at the Brownstone Building when the situation called for it.

Trey closed the door and dropped into a chair across from the bounty hunter. "I'm sorry about Lachlan, James. I should have seen that shit coming."

"You set him straight, and now it's up to him. Not everyone is cut out for this life. We've known that since I started the agency."

Trey frowned. "I swear, if that bitch causes any more trouble…" He sighed. "Whatever. Royce will whip his ass into shape. We need to focus on the barbeque team soon, too. Need to get some competitions and experience under our belts."

"Sounds good. I've done a few competitions, but I'm not an expert."

"You keep saying that. Doesn't make it any less bullshit."

James grunted noncommittally.

Trey shrugged. "Also it don't matter. Half the point of

this is to get the guys feeling good about shit, so I figure we want to play to people's strengths."

"We'll have to ask what their preferences are. Break 'em up by major sauce types. Maybe meat choices, you know? Brisket team, rib team, that sort of shit." James grunted and nodded. "A few guys per team, but multiple teams."

"You know the main thing anyone needs to improve their skills, right?"

James shrugged. "Practice?"

Trey snapped. "Exactly, big man."

"Then we'll need grills. Plenty of space out back. We can have a covered grilling area set up there. We should grill out at least once a week, weather permitting. Nothing in the permits that I've seen that says I can't grill out there."

Trey laughed. "I doubt the boys are going to complain about barbeque every week. It works as both training and a fringe benefit."

James grunted. "Didn't think of it that way."

"What about you, big man? You gonna be on a team?"

"Don't know. Maybe I'll be my own team and give bonuses to anyone who beats me at competitions."

Trey grinned. "At least beating you at barbeque is something we might be able to pull off."

Dannec puttered around his apartment, amused by how much money he was earning helping the LAPD AET. He'd have to save his favor for something important. Contrary to what Lieutenant Hall believed, no nefarious plan lingered in his heart.

He was a businessman, plain and simple. He couldn't help it if occasionally the laws of either Earth or Oriceran took a dim view of his businesses, but he wasn't a savage like the witch the lieutenant and her men took down.

The Light Elf clucked his tongue. His people wouldn't tolerate his return to Oriceran, but it didn't matter. He had a place on Earth now, and respect of sorts. Some might call it exile, but he preferred to think of it as a new opportunity.

A sonorous melody played from a nearby chime. Dannec spun and narrowed his eyes. He hurried into the hallway and threw open the door to his bedroom.

A painting depicting two smiling Light Elf children hung on the wall. He raised his hands and issued the melodic incantation required with ease.

Opaque bands of color surrounded the frame and then shot across and down over the painting. A glowing map of Los Angeles County replaced the image of the children. Scarlet and black bands pulsed across the image.

He sucked in a breath. "Drow."

Dannec gestured and performed another incantation, trying to tighten the location. The bands continued to flutter across the map.

"I'll give you that you're smart enough not to let me easily trace you, you damned Drow."

The elf dropped onto the edge of his bed, his hands tightened into a fist. Even if his own people had exiled him and he felt little loyalty to them, it didn't change the fact that he despised Drow.

Dannec took a deep breath. He'd learned many things

since coming to Earth, but chief among them was to not always rely on magic as a solution.

The elf rose and hurried into the other room to grab his phone. He dialed Tyler.

"Hello, Dannec," Tyler answered. "If this is about the money, it'll be a few more days. You know I won't fuck you over."

"Yes, you're not brave enough for that, but this isn't about that."

"Oh? What's it about?"

"I want to offer you some free information."

"No such thing as 'free' in my experience. Always a cost."

Dannec chuckled. "You're like me, Tyler—a businessman. You know what makes a *good* businessman?"

"A nose for profit?"

"Yes. And you know what makes for a good business environment?"

"Hmm. I'd have to say stability."

"Exactly," Dannec replied. "A certain amount of controlled chaos is useful at times, but I'm like you, I prefer a steady stream of predictable customers. It makes things less annoying."

"Okay," Tyler responded. "Did you just decide to call me so we can chitchat about business theory?"

"There are Drow in Los Angeles. From what I can tell, several of them."

"What the fuck is a Drow? Is this a good thing or bad thing?

"Dark Elves."

Tyler sighed. "Dark Elves, as in evil?"

"That, like most things, is a matter of perspective. The problem is, they are individually very powerful. It pains me to admit that the average Dark Elf is more powerful than the average Light Elf or Wood Elf."

"So they've got a lot of magic? That's not a big deal."

"They're not only powerful, but they are incredibly selfish and care only about their own people. Most other people are mere resources for them to expend. They aren't as bad as Atlanteans, but to put it in terms you might better understand that's like saying that the Italian Fascists weren't as bad as the Nazis."

Tyler laughed. "Tell me how you *really* feel, Dannec."

"This isn't a laughing matter, Tyler. The point is that if they are here, it doesn't mean anything good for anyone else. Even if they are here for something very specific, it's likely someone is going to be hurt or killed in the process. I'd heard rumors of them being in the area before, but I was out of town for some time on a business matter before my most recent encounter with the excitable Lieutenant Hall. They also might have been purposefully hiding their magical signatures."

"Huh. Okay. So these Drow are going to stir shit up and they are powerful, is what you're saying."

"Yes. Feel free to pass that along to whoever might find it useful."

Tyler chuckled. "I will, once I figure out how to make some money off it."

5

Royce settled in across from James in his office.

"How did everything go with Lachlan?" James inquired.

The drill instructor shrugged. "He's got a lot of attitude, but I dealt with a shitload of attitude during my time in the Corps. It's nothing I can't handle."

"Good. The more guys we can get up to speed, the better. Trey's doing a great job, but he's also only one man. The discipline you're instilling in them will help them go after bounties without the situation getting out of control. The hand-to-hand you're teaching them will help, since not everyone surrenders." James chuckled. "I've seen a lot of these guys shoot. They're more interested in looking cool than hitting shit."

Royce laughed. "Yeah, but at least they've handled weapons. That helps. I'm going to introduce proper firearms training next Friday. By the time I'm done with these guys, they'll be able to field-strip multiple weapons while under fire if necessary."

James nodded. "Trey told me everything's coming along in helping them learn investigation and tracking skills. Some of the guys might never be all that good on their own, but that's not a problem. They are used to working in groups, so we can pair or triple them up. I'd prefer that. It's safer."

"I agree. I get that we're not training a platoon here, but I don't want these guys running around thinking they are you."

James grunted. "Trey's got a good head on his shoulders, and he's helping to keep them in check. Not all that worried."

Royce crossed his arms. "Sure, but at the end of the day, it's the Brownstone Agency. It's important that these guys remember that."

"Huh?"

"In the Corps, we have centuries of tradition to help keep people in line, along with a Marine's love of his country. The Brownstone Agency is, well, like Trey was saying, it's closer to a gang."

"Yeah. I guess. What about it?"

"Other than Lachlan, I don't think there's a single man I'm working with who doesn't respect you or think you could do some serious damage. On the other hand, it's important in gangs to remind people of the leader's strength."

James frowned. "I'm not following you, Royce."

"The King of the Pit."

The bounty hunter shrugged. "I'm the King of the Barbeque Pit."

The drill instructor chuckled. "I'm going to be setting up two teams for the whole thing, but how about you work as Team Three?"

James shook his head. "I'm not trying to be an arrogant dick, Royce, but none of these guys have a chance against me. What would be the point of me kicking their asses?"

The Marine grinned. "Kicking their ass is *exactly* the point. It's a pride thing with them. The winning team will get a twenty-minute rest and then take you on in the pit. When you win, they won't feel bad because of your reputation and abilities, but they'll feel good that they even got a shot at the true king."

James shrugged. "If you think it's a good idea, I'm fine with it."

"Yeah, I know what I'm doing."

"That's why I hired you."

Maria glanced around as she settled in at the bar. It was rather empty, which was unusual for the Black Sun, but even a popular place had to be slow now and again.

"No Kathy tonight?" she inquired as Tyler walked toward her.

"Nah, she's off for the next couple of days."

The lieutenant leaned in and lowered her voice. "And how is everything going with your new business venture?"

"Things are coming along. Most of the paperwork is

done, and I'll be able to pay the elf the rest of his money soon enough." Tyler poured her drink and set it in front of her. "And you're sure this isn't going to be a one-off thing?"

Maria shook her head. "Bureaucracy's too damned slow. If there's one thing the shit with that demon-summoning bitch taught me, it's that no one seems to get how quickly the situation on the ground can change." She frowned. "Everyone just assumes we'll be able to handle it, or some asshole like Brownstone will come in and save the day. But what good does *that* do when people start dying? So fuck it. I'm going to do what I need to do to protect the people of Los Angeles, and if that means occasionally getting help from a shady elf, then *big fucking deal.*"

"You know what they say about the path to hell," Tyler commented with a shrug.

"I'd rather die knowing I tried than knowing on my deathbed people died because I didn't try hard enough."

Tyler rolled his eyes. "You know, Lieutenant, I like you because you're anti-Brownstone, and you help keep this place neutral ground, but sometimes you're *such* a cop. You seriously buy into all that 'protect and serve' shit?"

Maria narrowed her eyes. "Yeah, I do. It's why I became a cop."

"You know what I think cops are?"

"No. Enlighten me, oh great criminal bar owner?"

Tyler smirked. "You're just the biggest gang with the snappiest uniforms."

She shrugged. "Maybe, but any decent gang makes sure that other assholes don't fuck with people on their turf. So it doesn't change shit whether this is about protecting or serving or if this is just about me being mad there are assholes in my territory who aren't wearing my gang colors."

"If you say so, Lieutenant."

Two thugs in suits entered the Black Sun and made their way to the bar. One stopped and stared at Maria for a moment after ordering two beers.

"Got something on my face, asshole?" she challenged.

The man held up a hand. "Calm down, Lieutenant. That's you, right? Lieutenant Maria Hall?"

"Who the fuck is asking?"

The man grinned. "I know this place is neutral ground and all, but I'm still not dumb enough to give my name to a cop. Don't worry though. Me and my buddy, we're big fans."

The other man nodded and gave a thumbs up.

Tyler set the beers in front of the thugs, watching with interest.

"Big fans?" Maria echoed.

"Yeah. We saw it on television. AET kicking that demon witch's ass. That shit was off-the-*hook* badass."

The other man gulped down his beer and nodded. "Yeah, I haven't seen that kind of badass shit since the last time the news caught Brownstone in action."

Maria gritted her teeth.

Always fucking Brownstone.

The first man nodded to his friend. "Yeah, I know you AET guys took down some high-powered killer not all that long ago, but we didn't see that shit on TV like we did this one. That crazy witch was just offing people, so it even got me thinking, 'Damn, those cops are protecting our asses. I actually wish I *paid* taxes.'"

"Uh, thanks," she managed.

The cop blinked and looked between the two men, not sure what to make of them. She liked AET being recognized for their work, but at the same time getting praised by criminals didn't sit right in her stomach.

The second thug set down his beer and burped. "Plus, I know you've got that armor on and everything, but damned if you didn't look hot taking that bitch out."

Tyler nodded toward a table across the room. "Hey, the lieutenant's tired. How about you guys take it over there, and I'll send a free pitcher your way?"

The men stood and nodded.

"Never one to turn down free beer," the first man commented.

"Keep up the good fight, Lieutenant," the second offered. He gave her a salute.

They made their way to the table.

Tyler chuckled. "What's a matter, Lieutenant? You can't take having a fan club?"

"I'm not used to it, no." Maria picked up her drink and took a sip, still processing the encounter.

"The Black Sun isn't a bar for tech bros or dentists. We get a rough crowd in here, and rough guys tend to like their women with a little backbone."

Maria smirked. "So, what...I'm the pin-up girl for the Black Sun now? You have plenty of waitresses with short skirts."

"Yeah, but no backbone, and the average mob enforcer can't say he's taken on a demon-summoning witch." Tyler shrugged. "Take the respect people are willing to throw your way. It might come in useful someday. After all, AET aren't like most cops."

"What do you mean?"

Tyler gestured to the two thugs and then a lone gang member drowning his sorrows with a surprisingly expensive bottle of French wine.

"It's what I was getting at earlier. Cops aren't really about protecting and serving normally. They are about upholding the status quo. Yeah, yeah, they get criminals and thieves off the street, but the rich assholes at the top and the politicians, who are responsible for harming the most people, rarely get touched. Think about it. You think sending some dusthead to prison *helps* him?"

Maria frowned. "People make their own choices. They don't have to break the law."

"The law? The law changes all the time, and it can't even keep up." Tyler shrugged. "People break it all the time, whether it's using drugs, or speeding, or cheating on their taxes or some shit."

"You have a point, or are you just trying to piss me off?"

Tyler pointed at her. "To protect and serve, right?"

"Yeah."

The bartender gave her a lopsided grin. "Don't you get it? AET doesn't arrest people for using magic. Doesn't fuck with someone just for being from Oriceran. You stop assholes who have gone too far. It's like being a firefighter, you know? All you do is save people's lives." He shrugged. "Now, sure, sometimes it gets expensive, but magic isn't exactly easy to control."

Maria narrowed her eyes at Tyler, not saying anything for a long while. "Are you just fucking with me?"

"Nope, it's what I believe."

"What about Brownstone? Couldn't you say the same thing about him?"

Tyler's smile vanished. "Fuck that asshole. He's not a cop. He's a bounty hunter. He doesn't do it on salary because he wants to protect people. He gets a pile of money, and I'm pretty sure he gets off on beating people down. It's not the same thing at all."

"Huh. Not saying I disagree. Just surprised to hear someone like you say it." Maria polished off her drink and set down the glass. "Another, please."

"Sure thing, Lieutenant." Tyler turned to refill her drink. "You know, this neutral ground deal has done wonders for my business, but it's made certain things more complicated." He set the drink down in front of her.

Maria took a sip. "Like what?"

"Figuring out what music to play."

She tilted her head to listen. She'd barely been paying attention before to the classic hip-hop from the early 2000s.

"I don't usually pay that much attention to music in bars," Maria admitted.

"I have to. It's all part of the subtle atmosphere choices that help encourage people to spend more money."

Maria smiled behind her glass. "Everything's just an angle to you, isn't it? This bar, helping out the cops, having connections with Dannec?"

"Yeah, everything's an angle. The only person a man can ever truly trust is himself."

"I'm just asking if you can't just sit back and enjoy the music?"

Tyler laughed. "I enjoy music, but I can also think about how it can make more money for me."

Maria set her glass down. "What kind of music do you like when it's not about money?"

"I don't know. Classic rock, I guess, especially stuff from the early 2000s and 2010s. I like a little bit of everything though." He grimaced. "Not everything. Some of the Oriceran stuff I've heard, I guess I need magic or bigger ears or something to appreciate."

Maria laughed. "Don't have to like everything."

"What about you?"

She winced, regretting ever getting suckered into a discussion of music.

"I...fuck."

Tyler crossed his arms, a shit-eating grin on his face. "Come on. It can't be that bad."

"You have to understand. I was an Army brat, and my dad spent a lot of time stationed over in South Korea. I spent my years from eleven to thirteen and fifteen to seventeen there. And you know what they say, your tastes imprint musically when you're a teen."

He shrugged. "And?"

Maria averted her eyes and looked down as her cheeks warmed. "I guess you can say I'm into K-Pop. Always have been since then."

That got Tyler's attention. "I would not have pegged you as the type. Thought you were more a rock chick, or heavy metal. Maybe even country."

She narrowed her eyes. "Don't tell anyone, or I'll blast your dick off with a railgun."

Tyler barked a laugh. "All the secrets I know about you, and you're most worried about people finding out your music tastes aren't hardcore?"

"Yeah. Funny how that works."

6

A sultry voice came from the speakers of the F-350. "It's important to realize that men and women are different. This doesn't have to be a source of friction. Instead, recognizing and celebrating these differences can be a wonderful way for any couple to strengthen their relationship."

Usually, when James hit the highway he only listened to barbeque podcasts. However, he couldn't ignore that he needed to improve his dating skills as his relationship with Shay progressed. Shay had the experience of previous relationships to go on, but he was at a disadvantage since she was his first.

For everything.

This shit is too hard. Kicking that necromancer's ass was easy in comparison.

James wanted their next date to be special, but he was having trouble figuring out how to accomplish that. He loved Shay, but that didn't mean he understood her. If he did, he might be better able to predict how she would think and react.

Sometimes she could be blunter and less emotional than him, but other times the smallest thing pissed her off and she'd insult him. At least she didn't cry when she was happy, like Alison.

Why do women have to be so complicated?

"Ignore the reasons why men and women are different," the voice continued. "It doesn't really matter when you think about it. Whether it's society, biology, magic, or something else, the only thing that you can do as an individual is accept those differences to improve your relationships."

James grunted. Maybe women *weren't* so complicated. Maybe they just seemed that way because he wasn't one. That wasn't changing anytime soon so this relationship podcast might help.

Was Shay sitting around thinking about how difficult he was to understand? He didn't think he was. He'd spent his entire life focused on keeping shit simple. That simplicity had died with the Harriken, but it had to make him easy to understand.

Fuck. I have one warehouse. Shay has five. That says everything.

"In acknowledging the differences, also acknowledge your shared traits. The typical ways of distinguishing men and women lack accuracy. For example, claiming that men are logical and women are emotional ignores many scenarios such as every single man who ever got into an unnecessary fight because someone challenged him.

"Many men are prideful and react emotionally to any

challenge to their pride. They should be mindful of that when evaluating their own behavior, and women should be mindful of how to engage men while remaining mindful of such emotionally-linked issues as pride."

Don't think I've ever beat someone down just because of pride. Does beating them down to scare the shit out of everyone else count as emotional or logical? Fucking Harriken didn't get the message. I didn't want to have to keep coming after them.

Shay's more obsessed with being the best at her job than I am.

But we both want to kick ass, like during our last big date. Shay just didn't want to ruin her outfit. Guess I'm different because I don't care if I get a guy's blood on my shirt.

James scratched his chin. That wasn't fair to Shay. She'd made it very clear that she didn't mind a little blood splatter, and even had used that fact to contrast herself with assassins whom she considered "pussies afraid to get blood on them." Upon reflection, he decided the big difference was he never cared about his clothes, but sometimes she did.

Some major Mars and Venus shit right there.

They both had favorite handguns. He preferred a .45, and Shay a 9mm, but it wasn't like her gun was pink or some shit like that.

"Since both genders are emotional, focus on the emotional cues and how to best respond to them. One common problem for men is they misinterpret complaints from women. If a woman is complaining about her day, a man will commonly interpret this as her asking for him to fix it. She's just venting. Not every complaint is a request for a white knight."

Shay's got the opposite problem. We should have taken down that cartel a long time ago. Does it count as being a white knight if you take on a cartel army with your woman? I think she killed as many guys as I did during that.

James frowned.

Shit. Maybe I should have counted. Is it bad for our relationship if I kill more of her enemies than she does? Am I supporting her when I do that, or undermining her?

He grunted. She'd tell him if he was stealing her glory. At least he hoped she would.

"Another difference is direct instruction versus indirect instruction. This can confuse some men, as it is, in practical terms, the opposite behavior displayed during venting. In this situation, a woman may present something as a question or an observation, but in truth, she's making a direct request. She's trusting in her partner's ability to perceive her emotional keys and act on her implied preferences. Success in this can be helpful in strengthening the relationship."

Shay was straightforward with asking for a non-fancy place. But maybe she was testing me? Doesn't seem like she would. I did have to talk her into going after the cartel, so maybe that was indirect. She might be hiding some shit from me, but it's nothing big. She told me I was an alien, so what else is there to hide?

James grunted, thinking back on how they'd first interacted. He recalled Shay's insistence that he was gay. Was that some sort of indirect ploy, or had she honestly believed it? It was like she was ten steps ahead of him in the relationship, and he was always playing catch up.

I don't get all this shit. It sounds like I'm supposed to do the opposite of what I think Shay wants, but that doesn't make any fucking sense.

"Depending on background and environment, you and your partner might have different hobbies. These present good opportunities to strengthen your relationship, even if you enjoy different aspects of those hobbies. Merely sharing the activities will be enjoyable and prove your emotional investment in each other."

Does picking out international criminal groups to destroy together count as a hobby? I mean, I took down the Harriken because they were fucking with me, and with Shay it was the same thing for the Nuevo Gulf Cartel. I think we both enjoyed at least some of it. The explosives drones were damned fun.

James didn't get enough chances to use explosives other than grenades.

I like a good fight and Shay likes taking down assholes, but it's not like there's always going to be a group of assassins after me that we can kill together.

James thought that over for a moment. If he waited long enough, some newer assholes would show up to try and kill him. As long as Shay was in town when that happened, they could share the fun of taking them down together.

Saturday bonding over bullets and hitmen.

He worked through other possibilities. Shay had made it clear that she'd never be into barbeque as much as James was, so that didn't seem like a strong possibility, but maybe a few "couple's tomb raids" could be fun. She could do all the historical research, but they could share any necessary ass-kicking.

Even though Shay liked to keep a lot of details about her raids from him, he knew she was getting banged up more than she was admitting to. It wasn't that he didn't respect her skill, but he was the alien with the enhancement amulet.

Damn, though. That would involve a lot of flying. Fuck. Maybe she can find a few tomb raids in LA and Las Vegas?

The minutes flowed together as James' truck sped down the highway and the podcast continued offering relationship advice.

"Depending on your relationship, you might find that more or less time together can help you, but be aware that's highly situational."

What does that fucking mean? Anything? That's really fucking helpful, thanks.

James frowned. Shay had been all over him the last few days, but sometimes she didn't seem to care about seeing him for weeks. While some of that was inevitable given her profession, there'd been more than a few times he felt like she was actively avoiding him. He didn't know if that meant she was pissed at him during those times.

Why not just tell me if there's a problem?

Maybe the couple's tomb raids wouldn't work.

"Consider also joint activities with other couples and taking up new hobbies together as a couple that are independent of either of your existing hobbies. New bonds you forge as a couple provide unique support to your relationship."

James grunted. He didn't know a lot of married people he could hang out with, and he doubted Shay would feel all that comfortable going out to dinner with a cop and his wife. Taking up some new hobby was a possibility. It wasn't like either of them worked a nine-to-five job.

Fuck. Just need to figure out what. Maybe we could learn to dance together, or competitive shooting. We do it for our jobs, but not for fun. Take up MMA together? Even if that's not what they mean by mixed martial arts.

James ran through the scenarios and kept stopping on the fact that Shay was supposed to be keeping a low profile. She'd been "killed" twice, and even though they'd destroyed the Nuevo Gulf Cartel, that didn't mean it was safe for her to wander around attracting attention at ballroom dancing events or high-powered rifle competitions. Anything they did together would have to be low-key.

The bounty hunter changed lanes. His exit was coming up.

James shut off the podcast. Nothing the woman had said helped with his immediate relationship problem—figuring out where to take Shay that would be special for their date.

Men and women were different, and Shay was harder than many to understand at times. But she'd chosen him, alien parentage and all. That had to mean *something*, and he didn't want to spend too much time second-guessing it.

"Fuck it," James muttered. "I'm going with my gut. She fell in love with *me*, not some ballroom-dancing rifle champion. I've got to be me. Can't be anyone else."

Detectives West and Lafayette filed into their captain's office and took a seat in front of his desk.

Their superior crossed his arms and leaned back in his chair. "I'm still buried in a lot of paperwork over this Red

Eyes bullshit, but you said it was important, so I made time. What did you need, guys?"

West nodded to his partner and then looked at his captain. "We were discussing our manpower issues and how things went down with the Red-Eyes Killer, and how Brownstone helped."

"Yeah, a lot of bounty hunters are pieces of shit, but that guy's all right." The captain uncrossed his arms and shrugged.

"We need more of that kind of thing," West explained, "and I think the Brownstone Agency could help with other cases, normal cases. Lafayette and I think the department should hire them."

The captain frowned and shook his head. "Brownstone's a good guy, but he's still a bounty hunter, and the Red-Eyes Killer had a big bounty attached."

West shook his head. "It wasn't a dead-or-alive and Brownstone *still* took the asshole out. He lost out on most of the bounty to protect the people of Las Vegas. He even told us ahead of time that he was in it to stop the killer rather than because of the money."

"I see." The captain shrugged. "But that doesn't change the fact the department doesn't have the budget to hire someone like that as an outside contractor to help sweep up our small fry, and it's not like he's going leave LA to grab a bunch of level ones and twos for us in Vegas."

"You're not understanding, sir," Lafayette chimed in. "We're not talking about hiring Brownstone, but his agency. From what we understand, he's got guys working under him. Regular bounty hunters who go after regular guys. I figure we sweeten the pot with some sort of retainer and get some of these guys to help us in addition to the existing bounties."

The captain nodded slowly. "It wouldn't hurt to try. Even if we can't get Brownstone, just having his name attached will help. He's proven again and again he has cops' backs. All right. Fine. I'll put in some paperwork, and you reach out to the Brownstone Agency about it. See what we can get going."

The detectives exchanged nods.

Fuck the mob. They were bringing in the Brownstone Agency.

7

Lachlan's legs ached, and his lungs burned as he doggedly put one foot in front of another on the hard-packed beach sand. Every motherfucker in the entire gang was ahead of him, with Staff Sergeant Royce leading the pack, yelling another of his damned marching chants, and every bitch calling after him.

"Everywhere we go,

"People wanna know,

"Who we are,

"And where the hell we come from,

"So we tell them,

"We ain't the Marines..."

Everyone laughed and shouted, "Except for motherfucking Staff Sergeant Royce!"

The drill instructor snickered before continuing the chant.

"They don't even look mean,

"We work for Brownstone,

"Harriken-killing Brownstone."

Lachlan didn't join the chant. It pissed him off, but that wasn't the main reason. It was more his difficulty breathing that made him opt out.

I don't need this shit. I can prove I'm tougher than any of these bitches, but I'm not gonna fall down here. They'll think I'm a pussy just because I can't shout and run at the same time.

His heart thundered. His stomach continued to churn, and a full-out rebellion was brewing. The peasants in his stomach finally got sick of the aristocrats in his brain calling the shots, and he fell to his knees, puking up his lunch.

The other trainees glanced over their shoulders to find the source of the loud retching. Most of them continued, but four men slowed and headed over to him.

Damn it. Here come the bitches. I'll kick their fucking asses as soon as I'm done...

Lachlan threw up again.

Shorty was the first to arrive. "Come on, future King of Los Angeles. You can't be puking up your guts on the beach. I'm sure that shit is illegal. Po-po are gonna come over here and fine your ass." He laughed.

Lachlan flipped him off. "Fuck off."

Max, a tall, lanky bastard, was the next to arrive. "Just breathe, man. It'll pass."

Even back in their pure gangbanging days Max had always been an easy-going guy, and he was smart. Trey had even planned to send him to college to study accounting so he could better take care of gang finances. Trey had planned to expand their influence, but then he'd decided he wanted to be a clone of fucking Brownstone.

Yeah, Brownstone's a badass, I'll give him that, and he even lived in our neighborhood. But working for him isn't gonna make us stronger. You can't be a strong king by working for another king.

Lachlan struggled to his feet, then hunched, vomiting again.

I'm never fucking eating again.

Kevin and Russell, the last two to break from the pack and arrive, exchanged glances. The two were solid muscle and not breathing hard at all. That only irritated Lachlan more.

In fact, none of the people who stopped were breathing hard. They had all run miles, and other than the sweat on their faces no one would be able to tell.

Lachlan forced himself to stand up straight. "Come on. None of you fuckers are winded at all?"

Russell shrugged. "It's called conditioning, bitch. You think it wasn't hard the first few days for the rest of us? Most of the boys were puking a lot more than you, but Staff Sergeant has been pushing our asses. It's just exercise. If you do it, you get stronger. Easiest fucking bang for your buck you'll ever see."

Shorty grinned. "I was running before I even joined up with you bitches. I haven't puked from running in a long time."

"Staff Sergeant says I have a natural frame for running," Max explained with a shrug.

Kevin pointed to the group disappearing in the distance. "Just start jogging, Lachlan. You've got to man the fuck up and *do* this shit. If you can't handle a little run, how you ever gonna run down bounties?"

Lachlan gritted his teeth and pushed his legs forward. His stomach twisted, but there was nothing left inside. The next couple miles were going to suck.

"Fuck you all. I'm finishing this shit."

Lachlan sat on the beach, his knees pulled to his stomach and his head down. The men chatted amongst themselves, drinking Gatorade from the two massive coolers in the back of Staff Sergeant Royce's truck.

The angry trainee's legs ached, and his abs hurt from all his retching. He'd never exercised so hard in his life. He would never admit it to the others, but a small hint of pride over his accomplishment had taken root.

Fuck them all. I'll show them. I'm tough as any of these fuckers. Running don't make you tough. It's about your balls.

Kevin, Russell, Max, and Shorty all grabbed their drinks and dropped into the sand around Lachlan.

Shorty slapped him on the back. "You did it, motherfucker. Congrats. You ain't a complete pussy."

Lachlan took a small sip of Gatorade before speaking. "Why?"

Shorty looked at him. "Why what? Why you ain't a pussy?"

"No. Why follow Brownstone? Why follow Trey? We were the kings of our neighborhood. We could have been more, but now we're giving up our freedom to work for some asshole."

Shorty snorted but didn't respond.

Max stared at the clouds hovering over the ocean. "How many old gangbangers do you know, Lachlan?"

"Huh?"

"How many old gangbangers do you know? Like some dude who is still working the streets, but has a few decent wrinkles?"

Lachlan shrugged. "None."

"That's right. You almost never see old gangbangers or old junkies, because they die young. For a long time, I didn't care if I died young. I figured our neighborhood was a shithole and the cops didn't give a fuck, so I joined the gang because I wanted to make sure people didn't beat my ass." Max grabbed a rock and threw it into the ocean, where it landed with a big splash. "I didn't join it so I could get my ass capped by some Demon General over bullshit, or because I was in the wrong place at the wrong time."

"Being a bounty hunter ain't safe. All sorts of guys are gonna try and kill you."

"Yeah, but the difference is *we'll* be the ones planning when to go after a guy. That's hella different than some drive-by gang shit."

Lachlan snorted. "How many old bounty hunters you know, bitch?"

Max shrugged. "I figure by the time I get old, I'll have enough money saved that I can be the boss like Brownstone."

Shorty laughed. "Y'all making this way too complicated. Brownstone's a fucking badass. If you want to be strong, you follow the strongest. Staff Sergeant's badass, too. Even Trey's a lot tougher than he looks. I thought I was Billy Big

Balls, but Trey, Staff Sergeant Royce, and Brownstone proved to me I wasn't shit."

Kevin gulped down the rest of his Gatorade. "I figure why piss off 5-0 if you don't have to? They looking for excuses to bust heads, but now we're gonna be on their side and get paid fat cash for it. I can't wait to see the look on those bitches' faces when I stroll into the police station with a bounty."

Russell grinned. "I bet you we get way more women saying we work for Brownstone than saying we are some street thugs. Working for the Brownstone Agency means we get to be badass, but still respectable. You know what I'm saying?"

Lachlan snorted. "Who needs bitches?"

"My dick."

The others laughed.

Max took a sip of his drink. "You got a better plan, Lachlan? Even if you quit now, you're not starting up a new gang in the neighborhood. Trey won't allow it, and Brownstone won't allow it."

"What if I don't give a shit about their permission?"

"You got some nuclear missile hidden somewhere we don't know about?"

"Huh? What the fuck are you talking about?"

"That's what you're gonna need to beat Brownstone. Think about this, fool. He took out the Harriken. Not just *some* Harriken. *The entire damned group.* And think about King Pyro, that shit in the sewer from a while back. Hell, that crazy-ass freak in Vegas. You wouldn't have lasted five seconds against them, but he won. There might be people out there who can beat Brownstone, but you're sure as shit not one of them."

Lachlan frowned. He couldn't challenge what Max was saying, but the man's word did clarify something that'd been bothering him for a while.

"Don't you get it?" he asked. "The shit he can do, it's not just being badass." Everyone looked his way and waited for him to continue. "I'm saying he ain't *human*. At first I just thought his mama dropped him as a baby or something with that weird-ass face of him, but it's more than that. You know he's some bitch from Oriceran, or he's using some super-magic from them or something. It's changed him into one of them."

Kevin arced his empty bottle into a nearby recycling bin. "So?"

"What do you mean, 'so?' You want to work for some non-human freak? This is Earth and the United States, not Oriceran."

"He's got two arms and two legs. Two ears. He pays us and shows us respect. I don't give a rat's ass if Brownstone's a motherfucking *dragon* under that face. Oriceran's part of the world now. Ain't gonna do you no good to get upset about shit you can't change. If you had been reading Marcus Aurelius, you'd know that shit." He snorted. "You gonna run off to some other planet where you don't have to deal with them magic folks? Good luck, bitch."

"I'm saying that humans can only trust humans."

Kevin chuckled.

Max shook his head. "Brownstone has shown his respect for our neighborhood for a long time, and he's lived there a long time. Fuck, man, the guy goes to church and gives money to orphans. He's not some evil Oriceran dude waiting to drink the blood of puppies. He doesn't even pick non-bounty fights. He only went after the Harriken because those bitches killed his dog."

Lachlan grunted and looked at Russell and Shorty. "You two okay with him? What if he gets pissed someday and turns into a monster?"

"I respect strength," Shorty declared. "Don't care what he is, and, well, he ain't the Devil because he goes to church. Whatever else he is don't bother me none."

Russell laughed. "Monster? Bitch, please. Mother-fuckers blew up his house. If he didn't turn into Vengeance Dragon then, he ain't never gonna."

Kevin slammed a fist into the sand. "He did, in a way. He delivered the fucking *pain* to the Harriken bitches. He only takes down fuckers who have it coming. Shit, the Harriken kept going after him. They were asking to die."

Lachlan finished his Gatorade as he looked around at the other people. He didn't understand how they could be so easy-going about working for a man so beyond their reach.

He furrowed his brow and looked down. Maybe Brownstone's superiority *was* what was really bothering him. When he was running under Trey he'd always figured he could take control of the gang someday when he got strong enough, but Brownstone was a mountain no one in the agency could ever hope to climb.

"Doesn't hurt to stick around," he mumbled. "At least I'll get paid to exercise and learn shit for a while."

Shorty clapped him on the shoulder. "Now you're starting to know yourself, bitch."

Staff Sergeant Royce wandered over to the group, his face impassive. "You did good today, kid."

Lachlan bit down his first nasty response. "I fucking puked my guts out. How is that shit *good*?"

"When I joined the Corps, I was so fat they sent me to pre-basic training to work out and lose weight. I puked more in those weeks than I probably would for most of the rest of my life." Royce shrugged. "Being weak to begin with doesn't make you a pussy. Any able-bodied man can get stronger if he puts in the time. The military's been doing it since the dawn of civilization. You just need the will to want to get stronger."

Lachlan hung his head. "I want to get stronger, Staff Sergeant."

"Good." The drill instructor narrowed his eyes. "Remember, strength also comes from discipline."

"I'm not sure I believe that, Staff Sergeant."

Royce chuckled. "I saw a lot of action in my time in the Corps. Terrorists, insurgents, all that shit. You know the one thing I realized about why a Marine platoon usually won against some AK-wielding-fucking insurgents?"

"Bigger guns? Better grenades?"

"Nah. When you're going house to house or through some mountain pass, fancy toys don't help much." He shook his head. "Let me give you an example. I remember one time we were clearing out some insurgents from a village. Assholes actually got the drop on us, but in the end they were all dead or wounded. Only one of our guys was hit, and he survived."

Lachlan looked the Marine up and down. "You had better body armor or some shit?"

Royce shook his head. "Nope. Better discipline. The insurgent fuckers kept just spraying and praying. They weren't picking targets and calmly aiming. Our guys didn't yell and scream and throw lead in the air hoping to hit something. We broke off into our fireteams and took our shots when the enemy presented themselves." He gestured toward the men who were talking and drinking. "You know one of the big things that studying military history impresses into a man? I'm talking universal crap that applies whether you're using a spear or a railgun."

"I don't know. I don't read much."

"Discipline always triumphs. In most pre-modern battles, you didn't even see a lot of casualties until one side broke and ran. That was when they got cut down. They lost discipline." Royce loomed over Lachlan. "The Brownstone Agency isn't the Marine Corps. If it were, we'd be more inclined to give a shit about keeping you. For now, it's up to you to continue proving yourself to me, the rest of the men, Trey, and Mr. Brownstone himself. Today was a good start. Keep it up, and I'll make you into a man yet."

The drill instructor spun on his heel and marched toward another group of men.

"Bitch thinks he's so special," Lachlan muttered under his breath.

Shorty laughed. "He's a Marine. Bitch *is* special."

"He's not a Marine anymore."

"Nah. My uncle was in the Corps. Once a Marine, always a Marine."

8

Trey cracked his knuckles over his head. Even though he wasn't being subjected to the full force of Royce's training, he needed to participate today, and there weren't any bounties he was feeling for the next few days anyway.

Got to set an example for the boys, and it's not like Royce couldn't teach me shit.

He'd already been briefed on Royce's training plans, but he'd kept them to himself. The more surprised the men were, the more effective the training was proving to be. The boys had gotten too used to their old gangbanger lifestyle, and all the training was opening their minds as much as it was training their bodies.

The men stood in rows. Staff Sergeant Royce was in front, and Trey was off to the side.

Royce put his arms behind his back. "Yesterday we went over a live-fire exercise, and I learned firsthand why gangbangers can't hit shit. It's called aiming, dumbasses. The point of a fight is to kill the other guy, not look cool."

Everyone laughed.

"Today's focus is different. Weapons handling is important, and we'll keep that up with daily sessions going forward. Being able to fire your weapon at a large unmoving target is one thing. Hitting your target when it's moving or you're under fire is a different thing entirely." Royce marched over to a table covered in large black angular rifles. Several large boxes lay underneath. "James has seen fit to invest a lot of money into your training." He picked up one of the rifles. "This isn't a real gun, because shooting your asses would just mean I have to train a new batch of losers. That said, it feels and handles weight-wise like a real gun, complete with recoil and a loud ass simulated report, but it throws out a laser, not a bullet. We'll be using electronics to register the hits."

"So it's like Laser Tag?" Max asked.

Royce shook his head. "Half of training is developing muscle memory and instincts. The last thing I want is a group of men who aren't afraid of getting shot. You think just because you've scrapped with some other gangs you know combat, but you don't know *shit*. Real battle isn't a fucking video game. There's no respawn if your brains get blown out."

Trey crossed his arms and waited for Royce to explain the best part about the rifle simulators.

"You'll be wearing expensive suits in our new tactical room."

"What?" asked Kevin. "You want us to all look like Trey? I'm not down with wearing suits, yo."

The room filled with laughter.

Royce shook his head. "Nope, these aren't business

suits. They are jumpsuits lined with specialty electronics that interact with the rifle simulators. If a shot skims you, they'll vibrate. If you get shot, it'll shock you, and it'll hurt like a bitch. That way you learn to fear getting shot and don't treat training like a video game. If you don't drop within a few seconds, it'll hurt a hell of a lot more. Also note that once you're dead, you can't shoot anymore." He held up the rifle. "For now we're treating this shit as one shot, one kill. The problem in a lot of gun battles is that once you get shot, you can bleed out because you don't realize how injured you are thanks to adrenaline. I'm training you to not get shot at all, so you don't die in a stupid-ass way."

Concerned murmurs erupted throughout the room.

"This ain't gonna shrink my dick, is it?" asked one man. "All that electricity and shit?"

Shorty laughed. "What's left to shrink?"

"Fuck you, Shorty. I'm gonna shoot your ass first."

"Save it for the tactical room," Royce shouted. The room fell silent. "Today we're going to have two teams—a friendly team and an opposing force. The teams will be randomly selected by the program controlling the suits. Friendly team's suits will be lined with blue lights, and the OPFOR will be red. Today's exercise is easy. Team death-match. Eliminate all members of the other team." He pointed to the boxes. "Everyone, suit up. We've got a battle to conduct."

Trey grinned. "Let's see what all you bitches can do."

Two teams in blue- and red-lined jumpsuits marched toward the tactical room. Royce stepped up and tapped the code into the keypad on the side. The lock in the door clicked, and he pulled the door open.

"Everyone in," the Marine ordered.

Trey filed in first, followed by the rest of the red team and then the blue team, their rifle simulators held with both hands and treated as if they were regular loaded weapons. Gun safety, even of empty or simulated weapons, was something Royce treated as a zero-tolerance matter.

The tactical room was a darkened gym-sized two-level maze filled with blocks, dead ends, ramps, and stairs. Even though no one except Trey and Royce knew about it, smoke machines had been installed in the roof, along with massive speakers and misters in case they wanted to simulate different weather conditions. The jumpsuits weren't waterproof, but they were water-resistant.

Surprised James agreed to pay for all this shit. Royce is training our boys to be Marines more than he is bounty hunters. They are gonna be some scary-ass motherfuckers when all this shit is done. Fuck, most of them may even be better trained than I am.

Trey chuckled and pointed to a nearby black wooden block. It was more than sufficient to provide cover for a grown man. "You all know I've been working the job already. Guess I'm just a fucking prodigy, bitches."

The men all laughed.

"But that don't change the fact that I've made mistakes. A lot of times when you go after these level ones or twos they will just surrender, but then again, a lot of them don't." Trey slapped his chest. "I'll be real with you. I ain't told any of you this shit yet, but I took rounds in my chest already."

"What the *fuck*?" Lachlan yelled. "How you still walking? Brownstone do some voodoo on you?"

Trey snorted. "Bitch, please! Bulletproof vest. But let me tell you, it still hurts like a motherfucker when you get hit wearing a bulletproof vest. It bruised my rib, and I was lucky it didn't break."

Royce nodded. "Not only that, depending on what type of bullet or rifle enemy is using, the bullets might go straight through. Vests are useful, but you can't depend on them to save your life. Your typical anti-firearm bulletproof vest doesn't do well against shit like knives. Cover will save your life in a firefight. All that movie bullshit where someone stands out in the open and sprays without getting hit—it'll get you killed. Do I make myself fucking clear?"

"Yes, Staff Sergeant," everyone shouted in unison.

"Most of you will be working the job in teams, so this exercise will help reinforce that. Watch each other's backs, and don't assume that just because you see a lone enemy, they don't have someone providing them with overwatch. We've loaded this place with a lot of surprises, but today I'm not going make you deal with any of that. This is just the start of you honing the situational awareness that'll help you not have to depend on armor or vests. The best way to survive any battle is to hit the enemy and not be hit. Simple to learn, hard to master."

The drill instructor marched toward stairs leading to the second level. "I'll be watching everything. If you're hit, just go down. It'll hurt less. Everyone, you have a minute to get into position on opposite sides of the tactical room."

The blue and red teams rushed around the room, the men shouting to others as they took their starting positions.

Trey took a few deep breaths, his heart kicking up. Even though he knew it was just an exercise, the adrenaline was still kicking in.

Trying to ignore his heart, he sauntered toward the back. Rushing into battle to get shot was a dumbass move. He wasn't afraid of a little pain, but he wasn't a masochist either.

I wonder how bad this shit actually hurts.

"Begin operation," Royce shouted.

A loud shriek followed.

"Fuck," Lachlan yelled. "I'm already dead. What the fuck?"

Trey liked his odds, since Lachlan was on the blue team. The OPFOR were already one up.

"The king is dead," Shorty shouted from behind Trey. "Avenge him, motherfuckers, if you dare!"

A few laughs followed, but they were soon swallowed by yells and loud simulated reports from the guns' speakers.

"Shit," Trey muttered, his ears ringing. "Gonna need some ear protection if we're gonna do this a lot."

Shorty and Manuel pulled behind Trey.

"What's the play, boss?" Shorty shouted. "We don't have no flag or shit to go after."

"You watch my back, and we're gonna go forward. Get into their territory." Trey pointed his gun at a narrow hallway bookended by cover blocks. "On three…two…one."

Wonder what James would do? Fuck, he'd probably pick a guy up and throw him through the wall.

They rushed forward, keeping low to the ground. His suit buzzed as a row of men on the second floor blasted away, their barrels peeking over the wall. Trey squeezed off a few return shots, and one of the men took a blast to the head.

Manuel groaned and collapsed to the ground. "I'm hit, Trey. Tell my girl I love her."

Trey laughed. "Stay the fuck down," he shouted back. "I'll avenge you, brother."

Trey and Shorty made it to the hallway and flattened themselves against the wall. More screams and cries of pain sounded from the red team's side. He frowned and looked around.

Fuck. We bad guys are getting our asses handed to us.

The OPFOR was being annihilated, thanks to the careful high-ground placement of the blue team firing line.

"Need a fucking simulated grenade to clear those bitches out. Have to talk to Royce about that."

A red team member who'd been shot stood back up but collapsed screaming a moment later. "Motherfucker!"

Royce laughed. "I told you to stay the fuck down if you're hit. Dead people don't walk."

"What about zombies, Staff Sergeant?" the man shouted back.

"I don't think you want me convincing James we need to simulate decapitation."

Trey chuckled. From what the big man had told him, decapitation didn't even always work.

Time to bring the pain.

He nodded to Shorty, and they both rolled into the hallway on either side. Kevin sprinted around the corner, but fell with a screech as Shorty and Trey both shot him at the same time in the chest.

The OPFOR pair halted at the exit, again flattening themselves on either side. Trey held up three fingers. He dropped one, then two, then three. Shorty and Trey turned the corner to find Max and two other men waiting in ambush.

Shorty dropped to the ground with a grunt. Trey lit up the three men, who all collapsed a second later.

Now I'm behind enemy lines. Time to light some bitches up and earn me a simulated Medal of Honor.

He rushed down the hallway and up a ramp. He'd flanked the high-ground firing team. Six quick shots sent all men to the floor with hisses, grunts, and moans of pain.

Suck it, bitches. Trey ain't playing.

Royce, his arms crossed, nodded approvingly.

Loud shots and buzzing in Trey's suit alerted him to someone behind him. He spun and nailed poor Charles in the head.

"You Brownstone jackoffs can't take me down!" Trey shouted, his heart thundering. "You ain't shit. I'll kill every last one of you motherfucking bounty hunters, cut your heads off and send that shit to Brownstone postage due to tell him to never fuck with the Garfield Cartel."

Royce arched a brow. "Getting into it, are we?"

Trey grinned. "What can I say? My team's winning, and

these guys need to know the kind of assholes they might be dealing with. It's all part of the training."

"Oh? Your team is winning?"

Trey nodded. "Yeah, I just took down six bitches. How could I not be winning?"

"Congrats, but you know what they say about winning a battle but not winning the war." Royce smiled. "There are five blue team left and only one red team member. You."

"Shiiit…"

"Yeah, 'shit' is one way to put it."

Heavy footfalls sounded on every side.

Trey shrugged, an abashed look on his face. "Guess I shouldn't have shouted that shit to everyone and given up my exact position."

Royce laughed. "You think? Gloat when the battle's over, not before."

"Guess I still have some shit to learn." Trey sprinted for the center ramp as men came up on both sides, their shots narrowly missing. He leapt behind a cover block.

Go for the three, or go for the two? Fuck. What would James do?

Trey jumped up to fire at a man coming down a ramp. Jolts of pain zapped his chest, arms, and legs as the four other members of the blue team lit him up.

"I'm taking you fuckers with me," Trey screamed. "Fuck the Brownstone Agency!" He squeezed his trigger, but nothing happened.

Oh, yeah. The shit stops working after you get hit.

Another wave of shocks blasted through every part of his body, giving his mind nowhere to run. He fell face-first, his arms and legs twitching. Aches pulsed through him for the long moments following.

Royce made his way down the ramp, his phone in hand. He tapped at the screen.

"The suits have been disabled," he called. "You can all get up."

Lachlan shuffled over toward Trey. "I may have got shot first, but I wasn't dumb enough to keep standing, bitch."

Trey rubbed his neck. "Yeah, I hear that." A deep breath later, he tried to push off the ground, but his shaky arms and legs collapsed beneath him. "Fuck, that shit hurt so bad, I thought it was going to turn me white."

Everyone laughed, including Royce.

9

Charlyce sat at her desk in the Brownstone Building. She was still getting used to holding down a job again, but working for Mr. Brownstone and her nephew had made the transition easier than she would have expected.

Living on the streets had had more than its share of hardships, but needing to adhere to a strict schedule wasn't one of them. It also helped that so far she didn't have a huge amount to do; mostly helping keep track of some of the bounty and expense information. Occasionally she had to pass information to or from the outside HR firm. Once the rest of Trey's boys started going after people, she assumed she'd be knee-deep in work.

It's like a dream, but it's real.

A job, and a clean and sober future. It wasn't all that long ago that those things would have seemed distant and forever out of her reach, but her chance encounter with Dina and seeing her nephew on TV had changed everything. Some might claim that was mere coincidence, but she found it hard not to see the hand of a merciful God at the center of it. Now she had a second chance at life, and her family back.

She'd make sure not to squander it.

The desk phone rang, and Charlyce blinked. With the agency being so new and given the nature of the business, random phone calls just weren't that common. They didn't even have any formal procedures on how to handle such calls.

Mr. Brownstone was righteous and generous, but it was also obvious that running a business was a new experience for the solitary man.

We're all given guides to our tasks by the Lord. All I can do is support the man.

She glanced at the caller ID. The call originated from Las Vegas. She assumed that wasn't a coincidence.

Charlyce answered. "Brownstone Agency, how can I help?"

"This is Detective West of the Las Vegas Metropolitan Police Department."

Charlyce gasped. "Detective, it's good to hear from you again."

West's voice held a note of surprise. "Charlyce Garfield?"

"Yeah, it's me."

He chuckled. "I guess they weren't blowing smoke up your ass about the job offer."

"No, sir, they were not. Mr. Brownstone's been mighty helpful to Dina and me. Is that what you were calling about?"

"No," Detective West replied, his tone apologetic. "I hate to admit it, but I guess we got spoiled by his help. The department is interested in hiring the Brownstone Agency to provide support on a few cases. We understand that Brownstone himself is a high-level bounty hunter, but this is more about lower-level matters. It was actually your nephew or some of the others I understand will be working for the agency that we were looking to hire."

Charlyce picked up her pen to take notes. "You have bounties for Trey and the others in Las Vegas?"

"Not necessarily bounties. In some cases, yes, but for others, we want the manpower and reach in addition to the bounty hunting."

Charlyce sighed. "I'll be honest, Detective. I don't know what to tell you. I'm still pretty new around here. I'll have to talk to Mr. Brownstone and Trey about it and get back to you."

"Understandable. I can be reached at this number, or you can call the main department and ask to be transferred to West in Homicide. This isn't just about murders, though. I'm taking point on this because I'm one of the detectives who dealt with Brownstone before."

"I'll let them know, and get back to you with their answer."

"Thanks. That's all I ask."

The detective hung up.

Charlyce immediately dialed Trey and explained the situation.

His response was less than helpful. "Shit. I have no idea how we even handle that. I've been just grabbing bounties from the app or the website."

"You must have some idea."

"I've got nothing." Trey laughed. "You'll figure it out."

Charlyce dropped her pen. "Huh?"

"You figure it out, and get back to me with your ideas."

Charlyce sighed. "Shouldn't we ask Mr. Brownstone?"

"The big man is good at many things, but figuring shit like this out ain't one of them. You're the administrative assistant, and you're looking at our records all day. You're the best one to do this, Aunt Charlyce. Okay? Once you have an idea, we can go from there."

"Okay, I guess."

"Talk to you later." Trey ended the call.

Charlyce sighed and rubbed her temples. "Lord, give me strength."

An hour later, Charlyce's heart thumped as she placed a call. The phone rang once, twice, then three times. She half-hoped it'd go to voicemail.

A cheerful woman answered. "New Bethany Church, how may I help you today?"

"Hello, this is Charlyce Garfield. May I speak to Pastor Smith?"

"What is this concerning?"

Charlyce swallowed. "It's kind of a combination of a few things. It's hard to explain."

The woman's cheerful tone faltered. "I don't know that I understand, ma'am."

Charlyce cleared her throat. "I used to be homeless, and I stayed at the shelter Pastor Smith runs. I wanted to thank

Pastor Smith for all he did. I'm off the streets now, and I'm working."

"Oh, that's wonderful! I'm sure he'll want to hear this. One second, Ms. Garfield. Please wait."

An instrumental version of the hymn *Abide with Me* played. Twenty seconds passed before the line clicked over.

"This is Pastor Smith."

Charlyce took a deep breath. "Hello. This is Charlyce Garfield. I don't know if you remember me, but I stayed at your shelter for a few weeks last year."

"I do remember you, Charlyce, and it broke my heart that we had to send you away. I've often prayed on what happened, wondering if I did the right thing."

Charlyce was having none of that. "No, Pastor. You had your rules, and you made them clear. I was in a bad place at that time, and it wouldn't of done no good for no one if you'd let me shoot up in a place paid for by church donations." Her voice brightened considerably. "You don't have to worry no more about me, Pastor. The Lord has shined his light on me, and I've beat the drugs and the alcohol."

"That's a blessing, Charlyce. I'm so happy to hear that."

"Thank you, Pastor." She made nervous doodles on her notepad as she spoke. "I did want you to know that I've cleaned up, but I also wanted some advice."

"Anything I can do to help you, Charlyce."

Charlyce took a deep breath. "I remember you had a program there…the Hand Up Program."

"I still have that program. I was hoping you'd be able to make use of it before…the incident."

Charlyce let out a wistful sigh. "The past is the past. Now I have a bright future ahead of me in Los Angeles."

Pastor Smith sounded confused. "I don't understand. The Hand Up Program is in Las Vegas. I can't help you out in LA. I can call around and find a similar program in that area."

Charlyce laughed. "No, no. I didn't mean that *I* needed the program. I have a job, and that's why I was calling. You see, I remember how the Hand Up Program took people in the shelter and helped place them in temporary jobs with local businesses."

"Yeah, that's the basic version of how it works," the pastor replied. "Why are you interested in that?"

"I'm kind of trying to do something similar, except not with the homeless. It's a swords-to-plowshares-type program for former gang members, and I'd just like a little advice on how to set that up. If you have the time, that is."

The pastor chuckled. "I feel like the Lord is slapping me in the face and saying, 'Smith, get out there and shepherd wayward souls in a whole other city.'"

They both laughed.

Charlyce let out a sigh of relief. "Then you can help me? I don't know a lot about organizing this sort of thing."

"Then we'd better get started. Do you have a pen?"

―――――――

"Damn, that sounds complicated." Trey shifted the phone to his other ear as Charlyce finished explaining her plan.

The key elements involved requesting flat fees for expected services, along with options for bonuses in addition to bounty values. The agency would guarantee the department a certain number of workers, as long as the police provided them the previously-agreed-upon fees.

"It's not really that complicated," Charlyce told him. "We'll just need to keep track of the money flow from our accounts and the fees being provided by the Las Vegas Police. I've already got several of the forms and contracts printed and filled out for California, Nevada, Las Vegas, and Los Angeles. Either James or someone with authority will have to sign them, though."

"I can do that. James got annoyed with having to do a lot of this stuff. After he got back from Vegas, he went ahead and made it so I can handle some of the busywork on his behalf."

Charlyce laughed. "I don't know if that's a promotion or your boss just shoving work off on you."

"Hey, I shoved this on *you*, and you came up with all this. I've gotta say, I'm impressed."

"I took it as a chance to prove to you and myself that I can be useful."

"Hell, Aunt Charlyce, you don't have to prove nothing to me. I'll run this all by the big man, but it sounds like it'll work out. I'm gonna text you some funds. Not petty cash. Personal to you. Consider it a bonus for handling all this for me."

"You don't have to do that, Trey."

Trey chuckled. "I know I don't *have* to. I *want* to. If there's one thing I learned from Nana and James, it's that you go farther in life rewarding people for doing well than harassing them for doing poorly. I've got to for now, but I'll stop by later to pick up those documents. I'll see you later."

"See you later."

Trey ended the call.

Charlyce smiled at herself. She hadn't had that many issues since starting the job. Before today she hadn't even been sure she could pull things off if she ran into a real challenge. The many years she'd spent on the streets might have made her sharp, but they'd sanded away the skills she needed to function in a business role.

Or so she'd thought.

"I can do this," she whispered to herself. "Trey and Mr. Brownstone have given me the opportunity, and I'm gonna keep proving to them that I'll be nothing but helpful. Thank you, Lord, for granting me strength."

Charlyce let out an excited giggle like a little girl's and leaned back in the comfortable leather of the luxury car as it sped toward the orphanage. She hated having to wait a week between her visits, but she had a commitment to Mr. Brownstone and Trey before volunteering at Father McCartney's orphanage.

She eyed a pile of small stuffed animals she'd purchased for the orphans, and a larger teddy bear she'd purchased for Dina. Trey probably hadn't had that sort of thing in mind when he'd sent her the bonus.

That's for others, but I don't know about spending all this money to rent this car. Just wanted to see what it was like.

Charlyce leaned forward to look into the driver's seat. A shimmering translucent form floated in front of the wheel. When she'd contacted Currus customer service on their website, the nice woman handling the booking ensured her that the magic they used to drive the vehicles was completely legal and did not involve any ghosts. From what she'd explained, there weren't even spirits or anything like that. The car was enchanted to work better with existing auto-navigation systems, resulting in a true self-driving vehicle that could work in any conditions.

Although purely technological self-driving cars hadn't taken off, this kind of combination of magic and technology worked well in a few applications, even if it was expensive enough to keep it out of mainstream use. As a treat for a woman who'd lived on the streets for years, it was perfect. Luxury without substance abuse or gluttony.

The car turned a corner and slowed until it stopped in front of the orphanage.

"Uh, thank you," she murmured, unsure if saying something like that was even appropriate. She grabbed the two bags containing the stuffed animals and stepped out of the car. The back door closed itself, and the car pulled away as she made her way toward the orphanage.

Father McCartney stood outside holding Dina's hand.

The little girl broke free and rushed toward Charlyce, throwing her arms around the woman. "You're here! I'm so happy to see you!"

Charlyce smiled down at the little girl. "I'm happy to see you too, my little angel."

A few hours later, Charlyce smiled through her tears as she chopped onions. Cooking for others, especially after living on the street, made her heart soar.

There had been so many nights she'd gone to sleep on the streets with her stomach gnawing on itself. Knowing the children in the orphanage would go to bed with their bellies full thanks to Father McCartney and the donors—including Mr. Brownstone—brought a tear to her eye.

Father McCartney chuckled as he stepped into the kitchen. "Always grateful to have volunteers, but I hate to think that I'm working them to tears." His gaze dropped. "Ah, onions. That explains it."

Charlyce dried her eyes on her sleeve. "No, it's not just the onions. It's tears of joy. Maybe you find it silly, Father, but I've come a long way in a short time, and now I'm in a place to give back. It makes me feel very happy, because I never thought I'd be in this position."

Father McCartney smiled warmly. "Everyone should give back to the community. I, for one, am very grateful for your assistance. Even with all the money donated to this place, it's hard to keep up." He sighed and walked over to table. The priest plopped into a chair and set a phone on the tabletop. "The sad truth is, although Dina is young enough that she might get adopted, a lot of these kids are too old by the time they get sent here. So we try to do our best to make sure it's a nurturing and wholesome environment, and that takes time, money, and effort. Volunteers like you who can help with things like meal prep or playing with the kids are vital." He looked at the phone and sighed.

"Got a nasty call, Father?"

Father McCartney shook his head. "A problem with one of our older kids. We allow them to have phones. It's a necessity, after all, particularly for the ones who want to have jobs, but she was getting involved in cyber-bullying of another girl."

Charlyce sighed. "Enough hate in this world that young girls don't need to be adding to it."

The old priest ran a hand through his white hair. "Things have changed so much. I was born in the 70s, you know. I remember hitting up the arcades in Trenton and thinking video games were the most impressive thing ever. When I was growing up, bullying was old-fashioned. Face to face." He chuckled. "So much has changed. Computers are everywhere. The internet. Magic."

"You're giving these children a place to grow up where they know they're cared about. That's all anyone can do. Sometimes it works, sometimes it doesn't. I was loved, and I made my mistakes. I don't blame no one but me for them."

A smile crossed the priest's face. "I know, and I have my faith to guide me. So much has changed, but people are the same in the end. All we can do is our best to impart our good values to the children. If their hearts are pure, they can do their best to resist technological or magical temptations. Donations from people like James and volunteers like you are a javelin of light piercing the darkness."

Charlyce teared up again. "I'm just trying to do what little I can to give back after years of not doing nothing. You spent your whole life trying to serve the Lord. That means something."

"Oh, don't get me wrong—I'm satisfied with how I spent my life. It's just refreshing to be reminded of all the good people out there."

The door swung open, and Dina wandered in. "Can I help?"

Charlyce smiled down at the girl. "I need some vegetables washed. Why don't you go get the stool from the closet, my little angel, and we can make dinner together?"

"Yay!" The girl scampered into the other room.

Father McCartney rose. "You're a good woman, Charlyce. Thank you for your help."

She shook her head. "No. Thank *you* for allowing me to help."

1 O

James chuckled as he took in the well-manicured lawns and the expensive new-model cars filling Shay's neighborhood. Even after his home was destroyed he hadn't even thought about moving into a new area, despite how rundown it was. He kept his yard and home well-maintained—other than the occasional rocket-launcher attack—and he didn't want some busybody from an HOA telling him what to do with his own damned property.

He parked his truck in front of Shay's two-story brownstone. She'd purchased it before they'd met, just one of life's odd coincidences.

Today was a relationship maintenance day. The podcast stressed that the occasional surprise was good for a relationship, as was sharing activities. He'd texted Shay to tell her they wouldn't have time for a date to throw her off. She'd never suspect he was going to ambush her for a special Brownstone Date Experience.

I hope this shit goes well.

James marched up the path leading to her front door and knocked lightly. He waited. Shay never answered quickly, but it wasn't about her checking her hair or make-up; it was her security system and weapons. It wasn't paranoia when a person had dealt with hitmen coming after them.

The door finally opened, revealing the confused dark-haired tomb raider. "James? What are you doing here? I thought you said you were wrapped up with bounty shit for the next few days."

"You busy?"

"I was going over some prep for a job." Shay frowned. "I forgot to tell you. I'll be flying out tomorrow."

James grunted. Was his surprise already over?

This is what I get for trying to be all slick about this shit.

"But what about today?" James pressed.

Shay shrugged. "I could spare some time. Why?"

James nodded toward his truck. "I'm gonna go wait there. Make sure you're packing for trouble and meet me at the truck."

"Trouble?" Shay leaned forward and lowered her voice. "How much trouble we talking?"

"Nothing we can't handle and nothing that requires any explosive drones. Don't worry about grenades. I've got a box in the backseat."

"Do you have any sonic grenades in there?"

"No. I never use those." He shrugged.

"I'll bring a few." Shay stared at him, not bothering to hide the confusion on her face. "Even though I have no fucking clue what's going on. I'll be right back." She disappeared into her home.

James headed back toward the truck with a smile on his face.

Time for the perfect couples' activity.

After fifteen minutes on the road, Shay sighed. "Are you planning to tell me what the fuck is even going on? You show up at my house unannounced, tell me to grab gear, and then don't say shit about why or where we're going when we start driving."

James shrugged. He'd been thinking the last several days about his discussions in Vegas with the detectives and how they'd thought a woman who'd be with him had to be into danger. It made him think about the kind of fun that only he could provide.

Shay wouldn't have had the jobs she's had if she wanted to stay at home and watch movies about chicks marrying their best friends from small towns or some shit.

"I figured we could do something different," James rumbled. "This is a surprise date."

"Different? What's that mean?" Shay laughed. "Surprise date? You gonna take me to a barbeque place that has a slightly different sauce?"

James shook his head. "No, no. Just figured the more shit we do together that we're both into, the more fun we can have." He checked the mirrors for any tails or drones before turning at an intersection.

"Yeah, I guess, but what are you talking about here? His and hers massages? Why did I need weapons for that?"

Shit, I hope she likes this surprise.

"Leland Carmichael," James announced. "He's the surprise. We'll hit Venice Beach later, but the first part is him."

Even more confusion spread on Shay's face. "Who the fuck is Leland Carmichael?"

"A dangerous motherfucker who has a problem with women." James' hands tightened around the wheel. "Level-three bounty. He's a freelance asshole who specializes in arson and car bombs. He served a few years in prison for minor offenses, but not anything serious because he's good at covering his tracks. More than a few witnesses have conveniently died in fires or dropped their charges, including several ex-girlfriends. Leland gets off on smacking them around, you see. But the last one managed to get some hidden video and sent that off to the cops before she went into hiding. It was enough to get the bounty, along with the other evidence the police have on him."

Shay nodded slowly as she took in the explanation. "This guy's level three, but you want help?"

"I've got a line on him. This guy's known to have a lot of thugs helping him, and it's good to have another person, especially since I'm not using the amulet, and I thought it'd be fun to do together."

"So, in other words, your idea of a surprise fun thing for us to do together is to go attack some dangerous bounty with a little army?"

"Yeah." James grunted. "For most of the shit we've done together, I feel like I've been pushing in on your world, and I get how you might not like that. But I know you can kick ass, and I want to be more backup when you take him down. Hell, you can have the bounty if you want."

Shay rolled her eyes. "No offense, James, but level-three bounty money I could find in my couch cushions." She gave him a wide grin. "But it still sounds like fun."

James parked the F-350 up the street from the old warehouse. "I got lucky. My informant told me this is Leland's base for the next few days. Fucker likes to move around a lot ever since the bounty got issued."

Shay inspected her 9mm. "Probably a good idea. You never know when some crazy-ass bounty hunter and a tomb raider might come knocking."

James and Shay traded grins. They exited the truck and made their way up the street.

James tapped the silver frequency jammer on his wrist. "Killing any drone feeds, but he'll probably figure out we're coming from that."

Shay shrugged. "Big deal. It's not like this is a cartel meeting. How many guys we talking about, anyway?"

"He's got a dozen with him. I don't know the bounty statuses on them, so we should be careful about killing them. Don't want to make more trouble for Mack if I can avoid it."

"A little handicap for the game, huh? Fine. I'll disable

them without killing them. It's a good skill to practice anyway." Shay winked. "Never know when you might need to interrogate an asshole or use a guy as a human battering ram."

James chuckled. They closed on the rusted-out gate of the chain-link fence blocking off the warehouse.

Shay frowned and narrowed her eyes. "Oh, he's gonna be one of *those* guys."

"What are you talking…" James spotted the thin white line strung in front of the bottom of the gate. He walked backward and gestured for Shay to follow. "Guess it's a good thing I brought a few thermite grenades."

"Thermite? You were expecting something like this?"

James nodded. "Yeah. He's known for shit like this. Thinks he's a real clever asshole."

Shay snickered. "You really know how to show a girl a good time with the grenades and death traps."

"Well, it was either this or a movie."

The pair backed across the street. James tossed a thermite grenade toward the gate. The bright flame ignited as it hit the ground and a few seconds later, the flame ignited the hidden explosives, and the entire gate exploded in a shower of dirt, asphalt, and twisted metal, leaving a small crater and a half-downed fence on both sides.

Shay laughed. "Just how many explosives did that asshole bury there?"

James pulled his .45 out of his holster. "I figure we watch where they walk when they come out to play. That'll mark the safe path."

They jogged back to the gate, their guns at the ready. Three men burst out of a side door of the warehouse. Shay lobbed a sonic grenade at them before they even lifted their guns. The grenade slammed into the ground with a high-pitched whine and the men collapsed, groaning and clutching at their ears.

She looks so damn sexy when she throws a grenade.

"We need to—" James began, but stopped as Shay burst into a sprint.

The tomb raider rushed toward several large metal barrels near the crater and leapt onto the first one. Her legs spread apart for balance she pushed with both hands on the edge to gain the momentum she needed to hop onto a higher barrel. She jumped from the top of the next barrel toward a drainpipe near the door. The tomb raider was on the ground near the men before James could even process what she'd done.

A few quick punches knocked two of the men out. She yanked up a third and stuck her 9mm against the side of his head and snarled. "Point to the safe path, asshole."

The groaning man, his eyes half-closed, raised his arm and pointed.

"If you're wrong, you die," Shay promised.

He nodded.

James rushed toward Shay, using the man's information as a guide. A few seconds later, he arrived at the side of the warehouse without exploding. Convenient.

Shay knocked the goon out and dropped him. "This is way more fun than a fucking movie." She kicked in the door the men had come out of. "And at least we know this one isn't trapped." With a grin, she entered.

James rushed into the cavernous warehouse as two screams from inside tore the air. Two goons lay on the ground, clutching their bleeding legs. Shay spun, knife in hand, and planted her blade in a third man's thigh. She yanked it out and sliced at the man's hand, and he dropped his gun with a scream.

James ducked and rolled behind some crates when three men on the other side of the room popped up from behind a wall of boxes and opened fire. The bounty hunter tossed a flashbang at them and sprinted toward the boxes. One of the men broke cover to fire again, only to get a faceful of Brownstone's fist for his trouble.

The man flew backward and slammed into a pile of empty crates, which collapsed on top of him. His two friends brought up their guns, but it was too late. James grabbed the weapons and yanked them out of their hands before tossing them behind him.

James grabbed both men by the neck and threw them into a nearby wall. One moaned as he broke through the weakened drywall and slumped, unconscious. The other thudded against the wall and fell to the cold concrete floor before he lost consciousness.

Shit, I didn't even check on Shay.

He glanced her way. Shay crouched behind a box, a smile on her face as she reloaded.

Looks like she's having a great time. Glad I chose this for our couple's pastime.

A half-hour later, they stood in front of a locked office door on the second floor of the building. All the thugs in the warehouse had already been knocked out or fled.

Shay reloaded her pistol.

James gestured toward her face. "You've got some blood on your cheeks."

"Don't worry, it's not mine." She used her sleeve to wipe it off and smiled. "Better?"

"Yeah."

Shay's mouth twitched. "You know what's fun about this?"

James eyed the door before turning back to Shay. "What?"

"There's no millions of dollars on the line, no weird-ass super-magic weapons that will summon demons or upset the magical balance of power. It's not like we're even saving the world from some dangerous international criminal gang. It's just some dicks we need to handle."

James shrugged. "Before the Harriken, I didn't have problems with that kind of shit. If I went after some Mafia asshole or something *they* didn't come and kill my dog. And, yeah, sometimes the real treasure at the end of the job is just getting a dangerous asshole off the streets."

"Just saying. Sometimes it's nice to get a workout where the stakes aren't so high."

James nodded. "Oh, I forgot to ask you earlier. What was up with that shit with the first few guys? I haven't seen you move like that before."

Shay winked. "I've been studying parkour. A guy I know convinced me it'd be a good idea. New hobby with practical use."

"Oh, that makes sense."

"You could always come along." Shay snickered.

"Though the idea of James Brownstone doing parkour is hilarious."

James grunted. "I don't want to anyway. It looks complicated as shit."

Shay snickered. "Never change, James. Never change." She nodded toward the door. "Have a plan?"

"He might have trapped it. I've got the frequencies jammed, but if there's some mechanical shit going on, there's nothing the gadget can do about that. I'd rather not get you blown up on our date."

"Yeah, that would fucking *suck*."

Shay wandered away from the door toward the opposite end of the metal walkway that led to the first-floor stairs. "Go ahead and kill the frequency jammer. I've got an idea, but I need to make a call to Peyton first. Wait there for now and make sure Leland doesn't run."

James shrugged and tapped the jammer off. He kept his gun aimed at the door and waited. Shay's footsteps echoed throughout the warehouse until she left the building.

A minute passed, then two, then five.

Where is Shay going?

Something shattered inside the room, and someone yelled. A loud thump was followed by silence.

"What the fuck?"

The door swung open, and James whipped up his .45.

A smiling Shay stood on the other side. The back window to the office was broken.

Leland lay on the ground on his back, groaning. Blood was pouring from his broken nose.

"Just needed Peyton to check the layout of the place for me," Shay explained with a wink. "Maybe I should become a bounty hunter. I'm damned good at this shit." She laughed. "Maybe better than you."

James grunted. "We could work together. That way you don't always have to run off."

"I'll kill the fucking both of you," Leland wheezed. "Do you know who you're fucking with? You pissant bounty hunter trash."

Shay walked over to Leland and slammed her boot into his head to knock him out. She smiled at James. "Nah. This was fun, but tomb raiding's about more than just money to me. There're things I want to know about the world, and it's the only way I'll find them out."

James tossed zip ties to Shay to secure the prisoner. "Just saying."

Shay smirked. "My little Jamesey-poo miss his woman when she's gone? Don't worry. We can do some shit like this again soon." She pushed Leland onto his back and winked at James. "Nothing says 'healthy relationship' like time spent beating the shit out of criminals together."

***

James and Shay walked side-by-side down the beach boardwalk. Streams of people flowed around them, some on the boardwalk and some having their fun on the beach or in the water.

Shay nibbled on a churro. "You're not pissed that I didn't go into the station, are you? Me and cops don't mix."

He shrugged. "I know. Remember, the LAPD thinks the AET killed you. I don't want them to ask any weird questions."

"Oh, yeah. That's true." Shay snickered. "I die too much. Makes me forget. I wonder how many times I can get killed. I'm like a cat."

James spared a glance at her, still not sure why this beautiful and talented woman was interested in him, of all people. She hadn't known he was an alien when they'd first met, and from what she'd said before and what he now realized, she'd been interested in him almost from the beginning.

Shay punched James in the shoulder.

He frowned. "Why did you do that?"

"You've got this funny look on your face like you're trying to pass a kidney stone or something."

James grunted. "Just thinking."

"You should stop that. You're not good at it." Shay grinned. Her smile vanished. "What's crawled up your butt now? Everything okay with Alison?"

"Yeah, talked to her just the other day. Things are going along well. That's not it."

Shay took another bite of her churro. "I liked today, James, if that's what this is about. It was fun." She laughed. "And you pulling a surprise on me out of the blue! Huh. That's the greatest surprise of them all."

"Why do you say that?"

"When I first met you, you were the king of 'routine.'" She made air-quotes around the final word. "'Keep it simple, stupid,'" Shay quoted in a deep voice. "I was too afraid to even be in your place in case I messed up a napkin or something. You weren't the most...flexible individual, but now you're grabbing your girlfriend for surprise dates, and you have a kid and a new business. You're like a totally different man."

James stared at the setting sun and the orange-red sky reflecting off the ocean. "I don't know. Meeting Alison and you led to everything changing."

Shay tilted her head. "Are you upset that shit changed?"

"Nope. Shit changes. Always will. This time shit changed for the better instead of the worse. All I can do is keep living my life and hope it doesn't change for the worse tomorrow." James grunted. "Guess I should get you back to your place. You've got to head out tomorrow."

"No."

"No?"

Shay sighed. "I do have to head out tomorrow, but I want to stay at your place tonight."

Shay slid under the covers in nothing but her nightgown, her toned form on display, but her standard seductive smile was gone, replaced by an apologetic look.

James frowned. "Something wrong?"

"I do want to stay over tonight, but we can't do anything super-fun." She gave him a sheepish smile. "Not that I don't mind me a little 'Stone, but if we fuck, I'm gonna have trouble walking tomorrow and I can't risk that when I'm about to go on a job." She laughed. "I guess we'll see if the pelvic floor exercises help, but for now I just want to be held."

James held her a little tighter. "All I want is for you to be by me."

James smiled as Shay sighed and rested her head on the solid planes of his massive chest.

I get it now. Before I was just living, but I didn't have a reason. Now I have Alison and Shay.

Two reasons.

James pulled his F-350 back into his garage, his thoughts lingering on Shay. He'd already kissed her goodbye and taken her back to her own place. He'd made her happy his own way.

This shit could work. We could have a real future together.

He turned that over in his mind as he stepped out of the truck. Things had progressed quickly for him to go from entertaining the idea of being with Shay to having a future together.

It wasn't crazy. She knew his secrets, and she hadn't pushed him away. Fuck. He knew *her* secrets, and he felt the same. They were two outsiders, and they were perfect for one another.

He trudged into his bedroom. Not everything was perfect. He loved having her stay over, but she did leave things unclean.

James threw open the bedroom door and looked around. None of her clothes lay on the ground. That was promising. Keeping life simple and having an organized, clean home were related, but not the same things. He hoped Shay accepted that eventually.

The bounty hunter stepped into his bathroom and frowned. A few stray socks littered the ground, and Shay hadn't cleaned up her side of the sink after brushing her teeth.

Wait. This is the only place that's messed up. It's like she's marking her territory or something.

James chuckled at the thought. Maybe he could leave her socks on the floor. It wouldn't be the end of the world.

His phone buzzed, and he fished it out of his pocket.

"The Professor?" he mumbled.

Good morning. I need to talk with you in two days at our usual place to discuss employment opportunities. Stop by around nine.

James texted back. **Okay.**

Don't forget about your participation in the Bard of Filth competition. Just because you're still training for it doesn't mean you'll never have to participate.

The Professor followed with an emoji of a beer glass and an eggplant for some reason. Maybe Father O'Banion was already in control.

James scrubbed a hand over his face. The damned Bard of Filth competition was always hanging over him like a buzzard waiting to feast on his corpse. The passage of time hadn't dulled the Professor's appetite for hearing James spew filthy limericks.

"Fuck."

I don't know how to do this shit. It's bad enough that I have to, but I don't want to go up and look like a total dumbass.

James furrowed his brow. Plenty of singers didn't write their own songs. It was time to outsource the filthy bull-shit, just like he'd done with the magic in Las Vegas.

He'd thought about asking Shay before, but she was enjoying the whole idea way too much. Asking Trey or

Sergeant Mack would make things weird, let alone Charlyce, Royce, or Father McCartney.

No. He needed an expert on depravity, but one who could keep their mouth shut and who he didn't have to deal with on a regular basis.

"Fuck. I've got two days. I can find someone."

James had just finished another slice of bacon when a thought struck him, one so disturbing that bile rose in the throat.

Fuck. No. There has to be some other way.

He did know one piece of shit who could keep his mouth shut, but he didn't like the idea of going to him for help.

It'll just be this one time. I'll throw some cash at him, get his help, and give the Professor the performance he wants. After that shit, I'll never have to worry about dirty fucking limericks ever again.

James took a deep breath and texted Tyler.

Tyler, I need some information from you on the side. Willing to pay a premium.

A few minutes passed, and James returned to his breakfast until the phone buzzed with the response.

Sure, Brownstone. Come to the Black Sun tomorrow morning around ten.

James grunted. He had the feeling this was going to backfire on him.

Tyler put his phone down, threw his head back, and cackled like a madman.

Kathy looked up from the glass she was polishing. "What the fuck, Tyler? Did you finally lose it?"

"Nope. I've just got a good opportunity to make some money and fuck with someone at the same time."

"You're such an asshole sometimes."

"If it makes me money, I don't care." Tyler shrugged. "Where is the Bitch List? I need to make a few calls."

The brunette rolled her eyes. "I thought you said those were the ladies you didn't want served."

"Nope. That's my list of women who would pay money to see Brownstone."

Kathy groaned and reached under the bar. She pulled a small piece of paper with names written in careful feminine script. She slid it over to Tyler.

He scanned the list, his grin growing by the second. "Forty? What the fuck? Forty hot ladies want Brownstone? This proves how fucked-up and unjust our world is."

"It's more than that," Kathy corrected. "That's just the list of women I've recorded since you told me to start writing those names down."

Tyler paced back and forth, shaking the list. "This is bullshit. These women are drooling over that asshole freak when they could be with a real man who'd treat them right."

"How do you know Brownstone won't treat them right?"

"You heard about Brownstone dating anyone from any of your contacts?"

Kathy shook her head. "Nope."

"That means he's such a twisted-ass freak that once a woman gets to know him, she goes screaming away and won't admit it." Tyler slammed the list on the bar. "Whatever. I don't give a fuck. I'll get my revenge the best way I know how—by making money off the dumbass."

"I don't get it. How is this list going to make you money off Brownstone?"

Tyler grinned. "I'm going to text them all with a special Brownstone Date offer. I'm not going to guarantee anything but the fact that Brownstone will be in the bar at a certain time. Fifty dollars will get them the time and two drinks. Several of them will buy food and more drinks, so I'll make thousands off Brownstone's ass." He rubbed his hands together. "Fuck you, Brownstone. I win again."

The next morning, beautiful women filled the Black Sun. Most were in strips of cloth that could only charitably be called dresses, skirts or tops. Brownstone wasn't even due to arrive for another twenty minutes, but most of his fan club had shown up thirty minutes to an hour early, and most had gone through more than two drinks.

All the tables were filled, and more and more men had been streaming in as well. Somehow the word had gotten out about the concentration of babes at the Black Sun that morning, and men, both criminal and civilian, liked their chances.

Tyler couldn't wipe the shit-eating grin off his face as he counted all the easy money he was making off Brownstone.

Who would have thought telling Brownstone to show up would do better for me than offering two for one for drinks?

The front door swung open, and a uniformed Lieutenant Hall strolled in with a quizzical look on her face. She maneuvered through the dense crowd, frowning until she arrived at the bar.

Tyler pointed at a mopey-looking man in an ill-fitting gray suit sitting at the bar. "You, get up."

"Huh? Why?"

The bartender pointed to Maria. "Because the cop lady needs a seat. Now get the fuck up."

"Okay, okay, already. Hold your horses. Damn." Mr. Mopey Suit glared at Tyler before grabbing his beer and wandering toward the TV.

Maria sat at the bar. "You didn't have to do that. I'm not drinking. Just wanted to check in."

"Everything's fine," Tyler explained. "Has Dannec complained?"

"Nope. Just my first time involved in this sort of shit. Guess I'm obsessing a little." She shrugged and looked over her shoulder. "By the way, what's up with all the 304s?"

Tyler stared at her trying to figure out what that meant. He wasn't an expert on police radio codes and had no idea else the number might mean.

"I don't get it," he admitted. "304s?"

"You know," Maria commented, pointing at a woman in

a neon pink semi-sheer micro-dress and heels that were probably used for hunting vampires on the weekends. "Bangholes, chickenheads, floozies, fuckbunnies, huzzies, hoochies, P.A.Ps, sausage jockeys, sororstitutes? Any of those ring a bell?"

Tyler laughed. "Oh, yeah, sure. Them."

"Surprised you know so many."

He shook his head. "Not everyone showed up. I've got more. But I'm still not getting the 304 thing?"

"It's a ho-down." Maria held up a hand. "I know, very police of me." She frowned. "But please don't tell me you've decided to branch out into pimping. I tagged you as a classier kind of scumbag."

Tyler snorted. "Nah, never going to be a pimp. I wouldn't look good in the suit or the hat. This is part of a little joke I'm playing on Brownstone. Going to fuck with him a little and make some money at it."

"Oh." Maria looked back at the front door. "Screwing with Brownstone is something I'm always going to approve of." She stood and smirked. "I've got to get back to the station, but make sure you tape that shit. I want to watch it later." She shook a finger at him. "And I'm not paying for the privilege."

James pushed into the Black Sun, his attention overwhelmed by the raucous din and the sheer density of the crowd.

The place had gotten a lot busier since Tyler had somehow conned the AET into enforcing neutral ground status on the bar, but James had never seen it so packed.

It was probably this full when these assholes were betting on my life.

He took a few steps in and stopped. Not only had he never seen the place so full, he'd never seen so many women there.

Tyler starting up a ladies' night or some shit? This place is usually more of a sausage fest.

A chorus of squeals and cheers greeted his arrival, mostly from the women, but from a few men in the corner as well.

"What the fuck?" James muttered. "Did I walk through some weird-ass Oriceran portal?"

A busty blonde shot out of her seat near the door and all but threw herself at him. She wrapped her arms around him and pressed her breasts against his chest. He spun, flinging her off, and she stumbled on her tall heels, teetering for few seconds before regaining control.

"James," she purred, and batted her eyelashes. "I'm your biggest fan. I've read everything on Scourge of Harriken, and I'm an admin at Granite Ghost Groupies."

James grunted. "Hobbies are nice."

A redhead shoved the blonde out of the way. "I want to have your babies so badly it hurts." She spun around to reveal a shitty tattoo of what James presumed was his face on her shoulder. "You're my everything. You're the embodiment of what a *real* man is."

He shook his head and walked away from the women. Several other women stood and pushed through the crowd, like a horde of frenzied maenads all closing on their sacrifice.

Tyler stood at the bar, his arms crossed and a huge grin plastered on his face.

You fucking prick, you set me up. I'd pound your fucking face, but you've got your stupid neutral ground shit now.

"I want an autograph," a groupie yelled. She leaned forward to emphasize her ample cleavage and the pen inside. "You can write on these puppies."

"I don't do autographs," James rumbled.

Another woman threw herself in front of James and took a quick selfie. He stepped around her and shook his head.

The red glow from a small globe in the corner of the room caught James' attention, a video camera.

Fuck. God help me if I do anything on video that gets back to Shay. For that matter, God help any of these women if Shay tracks them down. I gotta get that handled somehow, but first I have to get through all these crazy women.

Twins in slinky black dresses emerged from the crowd. "Hey, James. Why don't you hang out with us?" they offered in unison. They batted their eyelashes. "We do *everything* together."

James scrubbed a hand down his face, unsure of what to do. It wasn't like he could punch a bunch of women for hitting on him.

How the fuck do I get them out of here?

"Hey, listen the fuck up," he bellowed.

Silence swept the room, and everyone focused on him.

"If you want to talk to me or get an autograph, go wait out in the parking lot in a line," he announced. "I'll be out in ten minutes. I'm not doing shit in here."

A stampede of horny hero-worshipping groupies headed for the door. James shook his head and continued toward the bar. A good number of men hurried outside as well. It wasn't clear whether he had crossover appeal, or if the men just wanted to hit on the women while they waited for the main event.

The bounty hunter finally arrived at the bar and stood in front of a smirking Tyler.

Tyler laughed. "Autograph session in the parking lot? They'll eat you alive out there, Brownstone."

"Fuck that shit. I'm leaving through your back door." James pointed at Tyler. "Because I know you set this up."

The bartender shrugged. "Oh, you're such a poor loser, Brownstone. All I did was tell a bunch of women who want

121

in your pants that you'd be here. Maybe I'm trying to be your wingman, asshole."

James snorted. "I'm sure you found a way to make money off this shit somehow."

"Not saying I didn't, but no one got hurt. Unlike last time you played a little joke on me, where it ended in gunfire."

"Can't prove that was me."

Tyler inclined his head. "Don't give a shit. Just saying, the ball's now in your court for a little return practical joke, and that shit better not involve you sending thugs here who don't know the score."

James grunted. "I'll make sure to repay you in kind, asshole."

Tyler's smile faded. "Whatever. I'll just enjoy this while I can, and I still made a shitload of money." He poured a beer and grinned as he set it in front of James. "On the house, Brownstone. Consider it your fee. I'll even give you five percent off whatever info you came crawling here to beg for."

James leaned forward and lowered his voice. "This is sensitive shit, and I know you hate my ass, but I also know you've got your own code, and you won't fuck me over if I pay you what you need."

Something approaching respect appeared on the other man's face. "Okay, I might be able to help you, but only if it doesn't mess with any of my other rules." He finished pouring and set the beer in front of James.

"I need you to point me at someone who can be funny and filthy at the same time."

Tyler blinked. "Come again?"

"Like performance on a stage, but not just funny and filthy. They also have to be good at poetry and shit."

Tyler stared at James like some Oriceran telepathy beast had shredded his mind. "You want a foul-mouthed and funny poet?"

James grunted. "Yeah, that sounds about right."

"And you came to me to ask this?" He continued to stare, waiting for Brownstone to drop the punch line.

"You claim to be the king of information. Here's the chance to prove it." James took a sip of the beer. Shit tasted watered-down. Big surprise.

Tyler crossed his arms and furrowed his brow in deep concentration. "Give me a second. This isn't the kind of shit people normally ask me."

"Make it under ten minutes. I don't want those women coming after me." He glanced at the video camera again.

"Yeah, yeah, hold your horses." Tyler pinched the bridge of his nose and sighed. "I know someone." He grabbed his phone out of his pocket. "One second."

He pounded out a text, a pensive look on his face. A few seconds later his phone chimed with a response.

"Anna Forsythe," Tyler announced. He rattled off a phone number and an address. "She's expecting you. She says she'll be home for the next few hours."

James grimaced. "A woman? But this shit has to be dirty. I don't know if I want to be talking about sex jokes with some strange woman."

"Get with the century, Brownstone." Tyler rolled his eyes. "Trust me. You want filthy, funny, and poetic? You're not doing better than this woman, and that'll be two hundred and fifty dollars, Brownstone."

James pulled out his phone and completed a quick money transfer. His dealings with Tyler during the gambling events had left him more than familiar with the appropriate addresses.

Tyler smiled. "Pleasure doing business with you, Brownstone."

The bounty hunter shrugged and started toward the hallway leading to the back door. "When they come back in, just tell them I'm in the bathroom. That should keep them here a while more."

Tyler waggled his fingers at James. "Bye, Brownstone. And fuck you, as always."

The bounty hunter gave him a friendly wave. His quick retreat brought him to the back of the building, and he sprinted around the corner and toward the spot where his F-350 was parked on the street.

"It's Brownstone," a woman shouted as he reached his vehicle. "He's trying to get away."

The entire pack of women pivoted as a single unit, all squealing.

James threw open the door and jumped in the driver's seat. He slammed the key into the ignition and turned the engine over. The engine roared to life, and he screeched away from the writhing mass of feminine desire charging him.

Fuck that. I'd rather face Oriceran monsters or magical hitmen any day.

James kept checking his mirrors. Not for the typical assassins or thugs, but for desperate groupies who might be chasing after him at high speed.

Fuck. If they got my license plate number, they'll start harassing me at home. Shay's gonna kick the crap out of them.

He'd play it by ear, but new plates might be in his future.

Twenty minutes later, James was no longer convinced he'd need to throw his truck off the road and barrel through some abandoned industrial zone to escape a groupie. He was ready to risk a call to Peyton.

I need to make sure none of that video of them hanging all over me gets out.

"Good morning, Mr. Brownstone," the hacker answered. "Who do you need me to find today?"

"The second-best hacker after you."

"Huh?"

"I've got something I need handled and I need someone good who isn't you."

"What the hell?" Peyton replied, all the humor drained from his voice. "Are you screwing with me?"

"Nope. I'll pay you for the referral, but it just can't be you."

Peyton snorted. "You know what? I'm going to be real honest here, man. I'm offended. I can't believe you'd call me up and ask me to find you a hacker other than me. I've offered you nothing but good work, and Shay can speak to what a badass keyboard warrior I am."

James grunted. The call was going about as well as he expected. "I don't doubt your skills, Peyton. Calm the fuck down."

"Then why am I getting sent to the bench, coach?"

"This involves a sensitive matter. Something I don't want Shay to know about, and I'm not gonna sit here and pretend what you do for me doesn't get back to Shay."

Peyton let out a long sigh. "Shit. Okay, fair enough." He managed a pained chuckled. "Obviously, you aren't as afraid of her as I am."

"Nah, I'm afraid enough, which is why I have to do this shit without her finding out."

"Sorry I had a hissy fit back there. Just have a lot of pride in my work."

"No problem," James responded. "So can you help me?"

"I'll send you some contact info." Peyton chuckled. "But, since we've already been over it, you do know that I'm going to have to tell Shay that you even asked about this."

"Sure, but it's not the same thing as you telling her everything or the exact details. I'm not stupid enough to think she doesn't have a few secrets from me. I imagine she'll understand."

Peyton laughed. "You still don't understand women, Brownstone."

"Some shit is too complicated to ever understand."

"Okay, sending you the contact info now. These people aren't going to give you their names until they've done their own checks, though. Just so you know."

"That's fine."

"Talk to you later." Peyton hung up, but James' phone buzzed with his message.

Guess I have some time for some more messages before I hit Anna Forsythe's place.

13

James' phone buzzed as he waited at a red light. He was only minutes away from Forsythe's house, and the upscale neighborhood filled with townhouses and condos left him confused. Anyone who knew Tyler shouldn't be living in an area like this. It didn't fit.

He checked his phone. His earlier messages to the hackers were all the same. He hadn't explained who he was, but had requested a working relationship. Being able to figure out who he was from his phone number alone seemed like a good minimum skills check.

Two of the response messages noted they were interested in working with the "great James Brownstone," but the third kindled his interest.

You're really *that* straight up? This is so obvious I can't help but think it's a trap. Use the link at the end of this message today at 4:00 PM on the dot, and we'll talk.

James frowned. The link would probably make his phone self-destruct or some shit if he tried to do anything clever. He had plenty of time until the deadline, so he'd leave it alone until then.

The light turned green, and he sped down the road. A few minutes of travel brought him to a quaint light-blue townhouse nestled in a row of other homes. He parked the truck and frowned. Everything about this place suggested the occupant was not a woman who could help him win a filthy limerick contest held at a bar.

Maybe I'm thinking about this wrong. It's probably some college woman. Shit, the Professor is a professor.

James walked up to the front door and pressed the doorbell. He waited, his arms hanging loosely at his sides.

The door opened, and a beautiful blonde woman stood on the other side. Her silver glasses, high chignon, stylish gray suit jacket and matching long gray skirt gave her an elegant, professional vibe with a touch of sexiness. Her smooth features made her look young, but something about the knowing look in her eyes made her seem older.

A few seconds passed before James realized her irises were bright red. No red lines or thickened blood vessels spiked through the whites of her eyes, suggesting the color was natural and not the product of alcohol or drugs.

"Anna Forsythe?" James rumbled.

The woman brought a hand to her glasses and touched the side of the frame, a curious glint in her eyes.

"When Tyler told me there was someone who could use my help, I didn't expect you, of all people." She had a faint accent, but James couldn't place it.

"You know who I am?"

Anna gestured inside. "I would hope you realize by now that you're rather famous, Mr. Brownstone."

"Not my plan," James mumbled. "It's damned inconvenient." He stepped into the house.

A minimalist design aesthetic marked the living room, with an emphasis on airy spaces and white furniture. James hated white furniture. It was too easy to spot dust and grime.

Anna closed the door behind her and pointed to the couch. "Please feel free to take a seat."

Now that he was sitting, James noticed a row of photographs of men lining the opposite wall, some young, some old. While the pictures on the right end of the row had obviously been taken within recent years, the age of the photos increased as he looked at the left, at least judging by the clothes and the permanent shift to black and white. Faded daguerreotypes gave way to small portraits on the end.

James pointed at the paintings. "What's with those?"

"All brilliant men of great comedic talent. The paintings include some performers from the late seventeenth and early eighteenth centuries. I'm surprised you don't recognize some of the later ones."

"I don't watch or listen to a lot of comedy."

Anna smirked. "I'm beginning to understand why you need my help, Mr. Brownstone. I'll note I have an interest in men of great comedic talent."

He shrugged. "Not a comedian, and I never claimed to be anything but a bounty hunter."

"Of course. Would you like some tea?"

James shook his head. "No, thanks."

The woman all but glided to the other end of her couch, her every step elegant and sensual in a way that confused

James. He might not understand women, but he knew when a woman was attractive. He normally didn't react so strongly, though.

Fuck. Does this count as cheating on Shay? I can't even ask her without pissing her off.

Anna sat down and crossed her legs. She laced her fingers together, staring at James with her red eyes.

"By the way, what's with the contacts?"

"My eyes, you mean?"

"Yeah. It's just a weird choice."

A thin smile followed. "This is my natural eye color." She tilted her head, exposing her creamy neck.

James shook his head, trying to concentrate. What the fuck was going on?

He shot off the couch at a realization. "You're not human."

Anna let out a sigh. "That, I suppose, is a matter of definition."

"You're some sort of succubus or some shit like that, aren't you?"

"Are you familiar with the leanan sídhe?"

Huh. Maybe she's a regular and knows about the Bard of Filth competition.

"The bar? Yeah, I go there all the time."

Anna laughed. "There's a bar called that? How adorable. Let me put it another way. Do you know what the bar is named after?"

"Yeah. A type of Celtic fairy. Kind of like a succubus, but they inspire artists, and most legends say that inspiration ends up costing the artist their lives. They live bright and inspired but short lives."

"I could quibble with the details, but that's accurate enough."

James grunted. "You're saying you're a leanan sídhe?"

"I don't like calling myself that, but that's the name humans gave my kind."

A leanan sídhe is gonna help me win the contest at the Leanan Sídhe. If this isn't a sign I don't know what is, but I still need to be careful.

James shook his head. "And you live in Los Angeles?"

Anna shrugged. "Why wouldn't I? It is a city filled with men desperate for artistic inspiration. And, oh, I've not been here long, only forty or fifty years." She laughed. "I do love this place, and everything's become so much easier with the full return of magic."

James locked his attention on the woman, half expecting her to jump on him and suck out his soul.

You better not have fucking set me up again, Tyler. I'll bust my way out of Hell just to track your ass down for revenge.

"What do you mean?" James inquired.

"I've been alive a very long time, Mr. Brownstone. Before, when most magic was gone from Earth, it was hard. Imagine always feeling like I was on the verge of starvation, and always having to hide my nature from suspicious people who'd destroy me without understanding me."

James shrugged. "So, what…you went and inspiration-fucked a bunch of men and took their lives in exchange? Am I supposed to feel sorry for you?"

"Something like that, yes." Anna held up a finger. "But if I may correct a misconception I'm sure you have, I never offered my gifts to any man without explaining the cost first. All freely choose inspiration over a long life. I've never misrepresented myself to any of the men I've helped. I might have hidden my nature from the common angry peasant, but I'm not a monster preying on innocents."

"Fair enough." The bounty hunter stood and shook his head. "But I'm not fucking you for inspiration. I already have a girlfriend, and she's possessive and has magic knives."

Anna burst out laughing. James frowned and waited for her to stop. It took longer than he expected.

She leaned forward and patted the couch. "Sit, Mr. Brownstone. I can assure you, even if I were so inclined, you're not my type. Also, I'll have you know that it's much easier these days. The price of my inspiration is less dangerous. A man can have his cake and eat it, now. He just has to put aside the occasional weekend or two for exhaustion."

"So you don't kill people anymore?"

"I *never* killed people. They chose to sacrifice one thing for another, and I only explained the situation so you'll stop thinking of me as a horrible monster."

James grunted. "Sorry. If it makes you feel any better, I'm not exactly a guy who should be complaining about people being monsters. But I don't get why Tyler sent me to you. He must have known I wouldn't trade sex for information, inspired or otherwise."

"Ah, but you don't have to." Anna gestured again to the photos and paintings. "As you can see, I have a type, and you have to understand what it means to inspire. I'm the muse, but I didn't put thoughts into their heads. Their own brilliance generated it. I just fed that brilliance. After spending hundreds of years around men of comedic genius, it's hard to not have absorbed some of the knowledge." She smiled. "I can give you advice rather than inspiration."

"In exchange for what?"

"A favor in the future." Anna held a pale hand. "I'm not involved in any strange criminal activities, but on occasion, because of my nature I can be targeted by unfortunate individuals. It'd be helpful if I could call upon the Scourge of Harriken in such a case."

James nodded slowly. He worried about having to explain who Anna was if Shay ever found out, but he had trouble being outraged at a woman who'd done nothing worse than survive. Plenty of artists turned to booze or drugs for inspiration and ended up dead. At least the fairy woman guaranteed results.

"Okay. Deal."

Anna clapped her hands together. "Wonderful." She inhaled deeply, and a warm smile spread over her face. "Tyler gave me an overview of what you were looking for, but it wasn't clear to me the exact context."

"I owe someone else a favor," James explained. "And this favor involves me participating in a dirty limerick contest at a bar."

Anna giggled. "Oh, I love you, Mr. Brownstone. Everything about you is delightful."

"I hate this shit. I don't get limericks. I just don't get what's funny about them, so I can't think of new ones. I have to, though. There's no way I can get out of this contest."

"Let me ask you something. What is humor to you?"

He frowned. "Jokes and shit."

"But what *makes* them funny?"

James shrugged. "I don't know. They just are."

Anna wagged a finger. "Nothing 'just is.' Now, there are various types of comedy, but since you're interested in dirty limericks, let's focus on wordplay. I'd argue that the fundamental basis underlying humor is a betrayal of expectations."

"Betrayal of expectations?"

"Yes. Although someone might anticipate where a good joke is going, the best humor surprises a person. People's minds crave order, logic, progression. A good joke tricks that by taking advantage of that natural order." She laughed. "Take a pathetic joke. Why did the chicken cross the road?"

"To get to the other side, right?"

"Yes. It's been drained of all humor by repetition, but consider if you'd never heard that joke. When the person told it, you'd try to figure out what complicated reasons underlaid the chicken's travel plans. In this case the answer is banal, but it could surprise someone because of the implication that merely raising the question implies some special importance.

"Same thing with knock-knock jokes. The audience will feel the tension of the unresolved question and know that something is coming, but the final play on words, if done well, serves as a surprise."

James rubbed his temples. "Is everything in life so fucking complicated?"

"Everything in life that's worthwhile is." Anna rubbed her hands together, a hungry gleam in her eye. "Which brings us to your dirty limericks. The rhyme scheme itself helps, you see. It sets up an expectation in the listener's mind. You're familiar with the rhyme scheme, yes?"

"Yeah, that I do understand."

"Does your contest have particular rules about meter and feet?"

James stared at Anna.

"I'll take that as a no. We'll just focus on rhyme scheme, then. Some purists might complain, but I doubt your contest people will. Anyway, the point is, the listener is trying to anticipate and autofill the final rhyme, but a good dirty limerick has a strong contrast between a clean beginning and a filthy ending. Maximum contrast. Maximum surprise." She half-closed her eyes, inhaled, and shuddered. "Nothing like that surprise."

"I still don't get it. What's so funny about sex and shit?"

"A good dirty limerick rides that liminal line between the sacred and the profane."

James groaned. "Now I'm completely lost."

Anna shrugged. "It's simple, James. In this society, we think of sex as simultaneously important, even sacred, and also as nothing more than animal-like fucking driven by the basest of instincts. A dirty limerick takes advantage of that tension and ambiguity to pop up with maximum surprise. It violates our societal taboos about what we should and shouldn't talk about. Does that help you understand?"

"A little." James took a deep breath.

His head hurt, but he could understand what Anna was getting at. Sex was important enough to him that he'd waited until his thirties to even have it, but he also drove past prostitutes selling themselves on the street for cheap every day and thought nothing of it. Sacred. Profane.

Anna took his hand in her soft and warm hand. "Let's try a few, just so you can think about the form on a deeper level. This is above your understanding right now, I suspect, so I really want to help you deconstruct some and make sure you know how they work." She cleared her throat. "Ready?"

James nodded.

"Jane came home after a year,
From her trip to a land that was near.
A place barren of hills,
Where she learned many skills,
From fucking men after a beer."

Anna stared expectantly at James. "It's not the best limerick, but it's a useful example. Why might someone find that funny?"

James furrowed his brow. "Because they were expecting something about foreign languages or shit like that, rather than some woman learning how to fuck better. It's surprising."

Anna snapped. "Exactly! Let's try another." She inhaled deeply.

"The professor is studying mass,
And he teaches many a class,
But he comes home from work,
Too tired to smirk,
And still fucks his wife in the ass."

James groaned. "Now that's just nasty."

Anna laughed. "Of course it is. It's a dirty limerick. But you understand the contrast? You certainly seem to understand the violation of the taboo line between the sacred and profane."

The bounty hunter dropped his head. In all his life, he never imagined he'd sit in a townhouse in LA discussing anal sex jokes with a Celtic fairy.

He took in and let out several deep breaths. "Okay, okay. I understand now. I just need some time to think about all this."

"Good, good. If you need any more help, feel free to give me a call, Mr. Brownstone."

James lifted his head and nodded toward the photos and paintings. "All those guys told dirty limericks?"

Anna put a hand to her mouth and snickered prettily. "Some of the filthiest you could imagine. Or in your case, probably *more* than you could imagine."

14

James was slumped on his couch, his head lolling back. Spending the last several hours thinking about dirty limericks had made his brain hurt, and reading about them online meant he now had scores of the damned things stuck in his head forever.

"Fucking Professor," he growled. "I'll get you back for this."

An alarm on his phone beeped, and he sat up. It was almost time to make the call to the hacker candidate. If he could hire someone useful, it'd at least stop one humiliation. That was the annoying thing about computers and the internet. They represented a problem he couldn't solve through the gratuitous application of lead and grenades.

James loaded the message from the hacker and hit the link. The link brought up a blank website with a numeric address.

"You're prompt, Mr. Brownstone," came a deep and

heavily electronically distorted voice through the phone. "I can appreciate working for a man who is prompt."

"I don't like to waste people's time, and I hope they don't waste mine."

"I'm not here to waste your time. I'm here to talk to you about the job."

James nodded to himself. "Here's the deal. I need to confirm that you're legit, capable, and very hard to find."

The hacker laughed. "You came to me. Doesn't that mean you already know I'm legit and capable? The fact you could even message me proves I'm already hard to find because I know you had to go to someone special to get my contact information."

"All I know is that you can send me a fucking link. You could be some douchebag kid in his mom's basement."

Another laugh. "Maybe. Does it matter?"

"No, I guess not, but it *does* matter if you can do what I need you to do. If you do, there might be more work for you in the future."

"And what do you need, Mr. Brownstone?"

"There was video of me taken in a bar called the Black Sun in Los Angeles this morning. The place is owned by an asshole named Tyler. I need you to find it and get rid of it. I don't know where the security feed from the bar goes, and some people might have videos on their phones."

"Scrubbing the net is hard, Mr. Brownstone."

"You saying you can't do it?"

"Just saying it's hard."

"I'll pay twenty-five thousand for the job."

The hacker chuckled, the electronic distortion making

it sound sinister. "I'm willing to do it, but how will you know I got it all?"

"Guess I'll have to get an even better hacker to check on that for me."

"As if." The hacker snorted. "I'll update you when it's done."

Maria frowned as she knocked on Dannec's door. An anonymous text on her phone that looked suspiciously like Tyler had written it had suggested that she stop by and ask the elf about "the new players in town." It had also told her to show up in uniform, so she had half-expected the wall to be missing a door when she got there, like it had been last time she'd shown up in cop clothes.

The door creaked open, and the elf looked her up and down, a faint smile on his face. "You look a lot better in your uniform. You command respect and exude authority." He gestured inside. "Please, come in and take a seat."

She brushed past Dannec. "I'm not even sure why I'm here. I think Tyler was trying to push me your way without giving away it was him. It's like the guy doesn't want to come off as anything less than a scumbag for some reason."

Dannec chuckled. "Reputations serve people in a variety of ways, but what's more important are results."

Maria sat on the couch and rubbed her fingers against her sweaty palms. "I was told to show up in uniform, but before it was always emphasized to me that it would be a bad idea."

"When you're doing things outside of the law, you

should not dress as a cop, when you're doing things within the law you should. Consider that a type of sympathetic magic."

Maria frowned. "What the exact fuck is going on?"

Dannec dropped into a worn recliner next to the couch with a sigh. "There are some unpleasant beings out there causing me concern. I should have talked to you directly before about them, but I was worried about my position. It's a good thing you're here now."

"What unpleasant beings?"

"Drow."

Maria shrugged. "What the fuck is a Drow?"

"A type of elf."

The lieutenant rolled her eyes. "Not exactly a rarity anymore, Dannec. Shit, I think AET has fewer issues with rogue elves than we do asshole wizards and witches."

"These aren't like the Light Elves and Wood Elves you're used to, or any other type of elf you've ever dealt with. They are a very powerful subset of elves, and they *only* respect power."

That had Maria's attention. "Why tell me?"

"These Drow are here now, in *this* city. You have sworn to protect and serve, have you not? The presence of these Drow means someone in LA is going to need protection."

"How are they different from any other douchebag Oriceran or human? Why do you need an AET lieutenant in your pocket to deal with them?"

Dannec leaned forward and threaded his hands together. "Let me put it in terms you can better understand, Lieutenant. In terms of destructive magical ability, the average strong Drow would probably be a level-five bounty, and some of the royals, level sixes."

Maria's eyebrows lifted. "Okay, so they are a little tougher than your average douchebag." She frowned. "Wait a second. Do they have a certain type of magic that they use? Like a certain style?"

He nodded. "Drow are Dark Elves, so their magic is forged of shadow and often fueled by death. While not pure necromancers, they can use souls and life to feed their abilities."

Maria shot off the couch. "Shadow magic? Like shadow swords and shadow wings and shit like that?"

"Yes, among many other impressive feats. I can't stress enough that they shouldn't be dismissed based on your dealings with previous rogue elves."

The lieutenant started pacing. "No, it couldn't be," she mumbled.

That bitch—what if she hadn't been human? I'm sure they could have used some sort of magic to change her shape and DNA. She'd had no artifacts on her. No wand, either.

"What are you talking about, Lieutenant?"

Maria stopped and spun to face Dannec. "You said they're here. How long have they been here?"

He lifted a shoulder. "I can't say. I'm not always at my place with access to all my artifacts, and depending on what magic they've been using, I might not have even been aware of it. They might have only been here for days, or it could have been months. The only thing I know for sure is that they are here *now.*"

Maria's lip curled. "Brownstone."

Dannec frowned. "Brownstone? What does he have to do with the Drow?"

"Not sure yet." She took a deep breath and sat back on the couch. "You said they respect power, and even *I'm* willing to admit Brownstone's powerful. Would they work with him? Maybe lend him some magical muscle?"

Dannec shook his head slowly. "It's not impossible, but it's unlikely. Their power is matched only by their pride. Helping an outsider—especially a human—would be out of character. If they have any sort of interactions with Brownstone at all, it's far more likely that rather than helping him, they want something from him—and it's not going to end well for him." He clucked his tongue. "Even the mighty James Brownstone may soon encounter a foe too dangerous for him to handle."

Maria gritted her teeth. "Wait, are you telling me that I have to fucking *protect* that asshole?"

The elf shrugged. "I'm only telling you what the most likely scenario is."

"Look, I came to you for the new deflectors originally because someone who we believed was attached to Brownstone nearly beat our asses. This woman looked like a human, but she used powerful magic that looked a lot like shadow magic to me. It was like she didn't think we'd be a threat at all." She pursed her lips. "Called us insects."

"She may very well have been a Drow in disguise. Sounds as arrogant as one. Since they only worry about power and the strength of their own people, the Drow aren't above underhanded tactics—assassination, imitation, and that sort of thing if it suits their own purposes. They aren't as bad as the Atlanteans only in that they've always been few in number, so they've been forced to restrain themselves or risk destruction."

"Great. Fucking perfect. Why isn't the consulate keeping magical terrorists out of my fucking city, especially if they have such a nasty reputation?"

Dannec's eyes crinkled in weary amusement. "Politics afflict Oriceran as much as Earth. We maintained peace through the Great Treaty with the ever-present worry of destruction looming over both our lands. A certain amount of tolerance has to be extended even to the more difficult elements." He shrugged. "It doesn't matter why or how they got into LA, only that they are here. Going after these Drow and neutralizing them, even if it involves protecting James Brownstone, will serve the cause of order in this city. Protect and serve. Doesn't that fit with your code of ethics and oaths, Lieutenant?"

Maria heaved a sigh. "Just what I needed."

"I'm willing to help with additional magic."

She shook her head. "I don't know if I can get more funds right away."

The elf held up a hand. "For free."

Maria blinked. "Free?"

"Yes. A short-term loss of profit is preferable to the greater one that will come if these Drow are allowed to complete whatever nasty business they intend."

"Fuck, *now* I'm worried. First things first—I need to learn more about them."

James opened his refrigerator and eyed the left-over steak

from the night before. His rumbling stomach kept reminding him that he hadn't eaten much that day and that it was time to remedy that issue.

Could go get some barbeque, though, if I can hold out.

He closed the refrigerator and headed into the living room to get his keys.

Barbeque it was.

James had just pulled onto the road when his phone rang. Once he saw it was from Alison, he switched it to speakerphone.

"Hey, kid."

"Hey, Dad," the girl replied cheerfully.

"Everything still okay?"

"Yeah, yeah. Everything's great, and I've been texting 'Aunt' Shay a lot."

James could swear he could almost hear quotation marks when the girl used the word 'aunt.'

What is that about? Is she pissed at Shay? Or pissed at me? I'm gonna leave it alone. The only thing more confusing than a woman is a teenage girl.

"That's good. Blow anything up with your fireballs lately?"

Alison laughed. "I wouldn't call my orbs and flames fireballs. You're making them sound more impressive than they are."

James chuckled. "Yeah, you're still building up to that. It's not like I could kick a guy through a wall when I was a kid. And your energy sight—it's impressive how much it's improved."

"Oh, sure. It's easy to see the energy of almost every-thing now. You thought it was hard to tell I was blind before, but now I think no one can tell."

"Huh." James frowned.

"What's wrong?"

What the fuck? How did she know?

"Why do you think something's wrong?"

"I can just tell," Alison answered. "You sound worried."

"Not worried, just was thinking how much things have changed for you at that school and how I wish you could have gone to it earlier."

"It's not your fault, Dad."

"Yeah, I know, but I guess it still bothers me."

Alison sighed. "Speaking of that…"

"What? Do I need to fly over there and go all Brownstone on someone?" He grinned at the possibility of intimidating someone on Alison's behalf.

Alison groaned. "No, that's the last thing I need right now, and it's not me you have to worry about."

"What do you mean?" James turned a corner a little harder than intended, earning a honk as his reward.

"I don't know how to explain it. It's like I can just feel something's wrong deep in my gut, and I know it has something to do with LA. Maybe it's because I've been training my magic."

James chuckled and changed lanes. His next turn was coming up.

"Alison, this is LA. There's always something bad here, especially if you count the politicians."

"Yeah, but I mean something magical and bad. Just be careful, Dad. I know you're tough, but it's not like you're invulnerable."

Nah, just mostly.

147

"Sure thing, kid. Everything's ready for summer break, just need you here."

"I'm excited to come home, but it'll be weird. I mean spending more than a few days in LA is going to seem really normal after spending so much time at the magic school."

James laughed. "I think that's the first time I've ever heard anyone refer to LA as normal."

15

James managed to park his truck in the lot of Philips Bar-B-Que when his phone rang.

"Busy day," he grumbled and snatched up the phone. It was from a blocked number. "Better not be another asshole selling fake Oriceran timeshares. I will track their asses down and make them pay for interrupting my barbeque run."

His stomach rumbled again, and he found himself again wondering how often that con was successful.

"What?" James barked into the phone. "I'm hungry, and whoever you are, you're fucking with my dinner."

"Has anyone ever told you that you're a rude asshole, Mr. Brownstone?" responded a voice. It sounded young and female; not a teen, but probably not that much older.

James rolled his eyes. "Yeah, lots of people, so get in fucking line."

"Damn. Do you need your diaper changed? Is that why you're so pissy?"

You're giving the groupies my number now, Tyler? Oh, fuck. What if he didn't, and they traced my plates?

"Who the fuck is this?" James rumbled into the phone.

"Based on what I saw on that video, I'm the person saving you from pissing off your boyfriend or girlfriend. However you roll."

"What the fuck are you talking about?"

She laughed. "Come on. There's only one reason a big, strapping man like yourself wants a video of women throwing themselves at him deleted, and that's because he's trying to make sure somebody else doesn't get pissed off. Otherwise, you'd be spreading it around to prove how your dick makes women wet from twenty feet away."

James grunted. That was not the conversation he wanted to have. Ever.

"So you're the hacker?"

"Yeah, you can call me Heather. I told you'd I call with an update. I did what you wanted. Your little meeting with the Ladies of the Brownstone Cult Auxiliary at that bar no longer exists. Because of how spread around it was already, the best strategy was just to nuke the whole thing. I was going to overlay footage from the previous day, but the cultists with their camera videos made that pointless. Doesn't matter. The point is your shame is gone, Mr. Brownstone."

Good. Shay's not going to go after a bunch of innocent women now. Being annoying shouldn't get you a death threat. Or a fucking death sentence.

"Okay," James replied. "I'll transfer half the money now, and the other half once I've confirmed with my other guy that you did take out the video. It'll be the morning at the latest."

"Fair enough. That everything?"

"For now."

"Good. Talk to you soon, Mr. Brownstone." Heather ended the call.

James grumbled about Tyler for a few seconds before calling Peyton.

"Want me to recommend someone other than my badass self again?" the hacker answered.

"No, I need your badass self to verify something. I had one of your recommendations do a little job for me."

"Hired them that quickly, huh?"

James snorted. "Yeah. Like I said, a sensitive matter."

"But you want me to step in on it now?"

"It should be okay. I hope."

Peyton gave a throaty chuckle. "Famous last words."

James ignored the taunt and continued. "I had the other hacker delete a video from the Black Sun when I visited the other day, and some other places, because there were some people with phones who recorded some shit they shouldn't have."

Peyton whistled. "Fancy. Hitting the Black Sun would have been easy, but getting the phone video from different sources required serious skills."

"I know this will take some effort, so I'll pay you ten thousand to verify the video's gone. Just check the twenty minutes after my arrival time." James rattled off the date and time.

"You don't have to pay me. I'm going to do this one for free."

James eyed his phone with suspicion. "For free? Since when do you work for free?"

"Since I want to see if I can find what kind of video would freak out James Brownstone so much he wants it purged from existence. Plus, I want to see if your little second-best hacker made a mistake. It's a matter of professional pride."

James grunted. "Whatever it takes. Just let me know." His stomach rumbled again. "It's time for some barbeque."

Peyton hunched over his keyboard, his fingers flying.

"Come on, asshole. I know you screwed up somewhere. There's no way you got all that cleared that fast."

He'd been inside the Black Sun servers and their offsite storage already and verified the deletion of whatever it was that Brownstone wanted hidden, much to his disappointment.

Leverage over the great James Brownstone might be dangerous to hold, but at least it was something. He still had a Deadman's Switch to protect himself against Shay. Having dirt on her alien boyfriend wasn't a bad idea. Even Batman kept some kryptonite around in case Superman lost it.

"Nothing? Come on!"

Peyton leaned back and ran his hands through his hair. He couldn't find jack shit.

So much for his kryptonite.

His concern over evil Brownstone, or at least a Brownstone who might come and punch him through drywall, was swallowed by his curiosity over the identity of the second hacker. The contacts he'd offered were competent hackers that he thought weren't as good as him, but he couldn't be sure. He only knew their online reputations and net handles, not the people behind the aliases.

The hard and surprising truth was that whoever had pulled off the mass deletion of the video was damned good. Maybe even as good as Peyton.

"But still not *better* than me," he muttered. He sighed. "Better text Brownstone, then let Shay know."

Peyton picked up his phone, brought it to his ear, then slowly lowered it.

"Wait a second. There's more than one way to get information. Let's see how attempt number two goes."

He grinned.

Shay frowned and pulled her phone out of her pocket.

"This better be important," the tomb raider yelled. "For all you know, I'm creeping through a dark alley trying to avoid a bunch of frogmen with laser wands."

"Shouting isn't stealthy."

"Fuck you."

The tomb raider glanced around the Bucharest alley she was standing in. The high walls of the surrounding buildings blocked out most of the sun, leaving the alley covered in shadows. No frogmen or any other supernatural threats followed her, but she didn't want Peyton getting too used to chatting her up when he got bored.

"I wouldn't have called you if it wasn't important," Peyton replied.

Shay rolled her eyes and leaned against the cool brick of a nearby wall. "Okay, then, I've got a few minutes. What's up?"

"To make a long story short, your man called me, asked me to recommend another hacker-for-hire, and used that hacker to delete some sort of mysterious video that was originally taken at the Black Sun."

Shay blinked. She pulled back her phone to stare at it for a few seconds before returning it to her ear. "What the fuck?"

Peyton sighed. "Yeah."

"Why would James hire somebody else to do that? He's got more trust issues than the next-to-last guy in a murder mystery, so grabbing someone new doesn't make a lot of sense."

"He told me that he couldn't use me because it was a 'sensitive' matter, and he didn't want me telling you the details."

Shay hissed. "Seriously?"

"Yep, but I'm telling you now what I know."

"I'm guessing you being you, you got butthurt over this other hire and decided to track that video down anyway?"

"James called and offered to pay me to track it down. He wanted to verify the other hacker had deleted it."

Shay took a deep breath. "Sure, but they fucked up, and you've got a copy now though, right?"

Peyton sighed. "Nope."

"*Nope?*"

"There's no trace of it. All I know is that for a few

minutes during the morning in the Black Sun, something happened that Brownstone doesn't want to get out. I sniffed around, and I found that Tyler sent out messages to a bunch of women advertising that James would be there. The son of a bitch was charging a bunch of money for two drinks and a chance to gawk at Brownstone."

Shay's heart rate kicked up, and she took several deep breaths. "Okay, thanks for letting me know."

"Do you think—"

"No," the tomb raider snapped. "Knowing James, he's probably head-tripping about me overreacting or some shit. Just because of a few little incidents."

"Incidents?"

"No one was hurt."

"Yet." Peyton yawned. "I don't have anything else to tell you, and I'm exhausted. I'm going to go ahead and let you go."

"Sounds fine. Thanks for telling me."

"No problem." He ended the call.

Shay sighed and slid down the rough wall. She pocketed her phone and shook her head.

James going to the trouble of hiring a hacker to purge a video associated with women did scream guilt, but wasn't like he'd participate in some wild sexcapade in the middle of a bar, even if there were a pack of Brownstone groupies around. He wasn't that kind of man.

Why am I so pissed about this, then?

Considering all the secrets she was keeping from James, including a few *about* him, she wasn't in a position to be outraged because he didn't tell her everything.

I did this to myself, too. I shouldn't have let him know that

Peyton told me everything about that lookalike and how he wanted it kept quiet.

James couldn't be a cheater. He wasn't wired that way. The man could have gotten tail before, but he'd saved his virginity until she came along, and that'd still taken her throwing herself at him and working closely with him over months to earn his respect and love.

Shay sighed and stood. "I can think about this shit later. I've still got a job to do."

The shadows shifted in the alley. She spun toward the movement.

Two men with wide grins marched down the alley, rattling off something in Romanian.

"Sorry," Shay announced. "I'm decent in a lot of languages, but have no idea what you said."

"Oh, American, eh?" one of the men replied in accented English. His ridiculous mustache almost made Shay laugh. "Tourist woman give your money, and we leave. Or we take money. Maybe you don't leave after."

Shay flipped him off. "That's my final offer, asshole. I am gonna be nice and warn you that I'm in a really fucking bad mood right now, so if you don't walk away immediately, you might be limping away later." She shrugged.

The two men glowered at her. Mr. Mustache charged without further comment.

Shay rolled her eyes. "For real?"

She sprinted toward the charging man, not going for her gun or any of her knives. Mr. Mustache reached out to grab her, and she repaid him by spinning out of his grasp and throat-punching him.

The would-be mugger fell to the ground, gasping for

breath. His friend charged, but Shay ducked the man's punch and pounded two quick blows into his stomach. He doubled over, and the tomb raider took the opportunity to slam his head into the nearby brick wall.

The mugger slid down the wall, leaving a smear of blood.

Shay kicked both men in the stomach, and they both groaned.

"Next time, assholes, just keep walking. You're lucky I'm the kinder, gentler version of me these days. Otherwise, you'd be dead." She smiled and glanced down at her clothes. No bloodstains. Always so hard to get failed-mugger stains off one's clothes.

"Huh. I do feel better after that." Shay walked out of the alley, humming to herself.

James was brushing his teeth in the morning when he decided to send the other half of the payment to Heather, assuming that was her real name. He tapped the Send button, and his phone buzzed with a message less than a second after.

Pleasure doing business with you, Mr. Brownstone.

He stared at the phone. There'd been no lag between his money transfer and Heather's response. It was as if she'd been watching him and knew what he was doing.

Shit? Is she in my accounts already?

1 6

Maria pushed into the Black Sun early in the morning. The staff were still pulling down chairs and setting things up. Tyler stood behind the bar, towel in hand, inspecting the glasses.

For a guy who wants to be a big information broker, he sure puts a lot of effort into this place.

She strolled up to the bar. "Send any interesting messages the other day?"

Tyler finished wiping the glass in his hand and turned to face her. "I send a lot of interesting messages. Is that why you're here, to talk about messages?"

You really just don't want to admit it was you, do you? Fine, I'll play along.

"Nope," Maria answered. "Just wanted to confirm everything's set up with your new side-business. I want to make sure Dannec gets his money as soon as possible."

He picked up the next glass and began polishing. "Why the sudden concern?"

Maria slipped onto a stool. "Dannec made me aware of some potential trouble that may be in town. He seems interested in helping out, but I want to make sure I stay on his good side. Especially if what he told me about this new source of trouble is true."

Tyler nodded. "Don't worry, the rest of the money should be transferred by tonight. Oh, by the way, I'm going to pass along a freebie to you."

"Oh, why so generous?"

"Because it involves our least favorite bounty hunter."

Maria snorted. "Of course it does. What about Brownstone?"

"Three more groupies showed up the other night looking for him, two women and a man. Weird vibe around them. I don't think they were the standard groupies. They weren't all dressed sexy, but more like business douches."

"Can be a fan without being some sex-starved groupie."

Tyler shook his head. "Don't know, but I trust my instincts. There was something off about them, so I mostly played dumb when they asked me about Brownstone."

"Did they say anything about who they are? What they were interested in?"

"Nope. Just that they wanted to know if I could give them any information on Brownstone. What he was like, that sort of thing."

Maria whipped out her phone. "Got video? I could run them through facial ID."

"Sure. One sec." Tyler grabbed a tablet from a drawer underneath the bar. He unlocked it with his thumb and swiped to his security app. He tapped away until he found the main security camera feed. After fast-forwarding, he hit play.

Maria narrowed her eyes. "What the hell is that?"

Tyler frowned down at the screen. In the video, the bartender stood there clearly talking, but instead of the three business douches, there was only hazy air. He rewound the video and played it again. No better luck.

He downloaded a backup copy from offsite storage and played that.

Still nothing but hazy air.

The bartender gritted his teeth and clenched his hands into fists. "What the fuck? This looks like magic. I guess they weren't just business assholes, then."

"Looks like someone got one over on you, Tyler." Maria stood to leave. "Let me know if they come back in, and I'll send some guys by just to ask them a few questions. I've got a few other things I need to check on this morning. See you around."

"Yeah, see you around." Tyler gave her a shallow nod, his gaze still fixed on the tablet. Those fucktards had come into his bar and used magic to screw with him.

I hope you fuckers do *find Brownstone, and I hope he tears you a new asshole.*

Maria waved and headed toward the door. Tyler's eyes widened at another painful possibility.

He rewound his video feed to before Brownstone's arrival the morning before. This time there was nothing but a frozen image from two minutes before the bounty hunter entered the Black Sun. The video stream unfroze if he moved ahead a half hour, but the intervening footage never displayed.

Tyler took several deep breaths as he tried to resist the urge to smash the tablet against the bar.

What the fuck does this even mean? *Did Brownstone do all this? Is this his revenge, fucking with my surveillance feed?*

Tyler face-palmed and set his elbows on the bar. After a long moment of self-pity, he returned his attention to the tablet and spent a few minutes checking the surveillance feed at different times of the day. The Brownstone portions were a total loss, and the mysterious trio had been redacted somehow, but he couldn't find any other portion of the video that looked altered.

Brownstone had every reason in the world to cut himself out of the surveillance footage, but he had no reason to mess with the images of the three assholes. They'd wandered in looking for information about Brownstone, and if they'd heard on the net about his appearance at the Black Sun, they'd know which footage to tamper with.

"So, which is it, Brownstone? Do you have some magical groupies who are trying to protect you or some assholes who are getting ready to waste your ass?" Tyler blew out a breath. "I don't even feel like setting up a pool."

***

Maria sat behind a massive blue crystal table, a twenty-year-old book and a tablet in front of her.

The consulate staffer, a pale Light Elf, offered her a smile from another seat. "Drow, you say?"

"Yes, Drow. Dark Elves. I know they're in town, and you need to provide me with information on them. Maybe I should talk to the consul directly."

"Unfortunately, that won't be possible, Lieutenant. Although we value our close working relationship with the LAPD, the consul is unfortunately very busy at the moment. I will, of course, offer any assistance or consulate resources you need."

Maria frowned. "I don't need consulate resources, I need information."

"About Drow?"

"Yes, about Drow. Not only do I believe several Drow are in the city and up to no good, but I also have some evidence to suggest a previous attack on my AET team was conducted by a Drow."

The Light Elf let out a merry laugh. "I highly doubt that, Lieutenant. Now, anyone in the consulate would be the first to admit the Drow can be very...feisty at times, but I can assure you that if we were aware of any dangerous individuals in the city, we would inform the human authorities immediately."

Maria flipped open the book and tapped a picture of a dark-skinned, white-haired woman with pointed ears. "Look, this is what I'm reduced to, going through a Dungeon and Dragons *Monster Manual* for information on Drow. If normal human legends are bullshit, the last thing I'm going to trust is what some game has to say about them."

She pushed the tablet toward the elf. It was displaying a page filled with artistic renditions similar to the one in the

Monster Manual. "But I need to know if this is who is in my town."

The elf took a deep breath and slowly let it out. "I can assure you that *I'm* not personally aware of any Drow in this town, and if the consul were aware, I would be as well."

"Okay, let's assume that's true. I still need to know about the Drow."

A look of discomfort passed over his face. "As I said, I am not aware that any are in town, but I will admit that Drow are very powerful, very selfish, very touchy, and very much a pain in the ass. I—and the consul, I can assure you —wouldn't want them around any more than you do."

"The consulate recently helped facilitate a payment to the department and AET following a pretty nasty incident."

"Yes, and?"

"We appreciated the gesture, but some new information has come to light about the incident that I think you'd find of interest."

The elf folded his hands in front of him. "Oh?"

Maria marveled at how the man could keep a smile plastered on his face ninety-nine percent of the time.

"The woman who attacked my team used a lot of shadow magic—shadow blades, shadow wings, that sort of thing. It's possible that what we thought was a rogue human witch might have been a Drow in disguise."

The elf's smile didn't waver. "That's a possibility, I suppose. What you describe is certainly consistent with the kind of magic they use, but it's by no means a certainty." He pushed the book and the tablet back to the AET officer.

Maria sighed and rose. She collected her items. "If you

FIGHT FIRE WITH FIRE

become aware of anything concerning the Drow, please contact the LAPD. I'm no expert in politics, but after the farmer's market incident people are on edge. Even though that was a human, a bad incident involving an Oriceran could make things uncomfortable for everyone."

Yeah, sweat a little, dickhead.

The staffer smiled. "I'll pass that message along to the consul, Lieutenant."

"Thanks." Maria headed out of the room.

After the door closed, the air shimmered, and the consul appeared. He sighed and shook his head.

"I'd thought we'd contained this, but now the human authorities all but know the truth about the Drow assassin. This is a disaster."

His staffer looked at him. "I'm sorry I couldn't do a better job of redirecting her."

"It's not your fault. It's Laena and her damned Drow, but if the police are poking around now, that means the Drow are likely up to something far more pernicious than mere mischief. We need to handle this issue ourselves before Lieutenant Hall and her people discover the truth."

The consul rubbed his chin. It was time to send a few people out there to sniff around.

James nodded to Trey across his desk. "Your message said you wanted to talk about the Vegas shit."

"Yeah, after talking with Aunt Charlyce and following up with the Vegas cops, this isn't just a request for some short-term temporary help. To make this work, we're gonna have to open an office in Las Vegas."

James grimaced. "Going from LA to Vegas is four to five hours on a good day. Not like we can have guys driving that shit daily. They'll have to stay at least a day to get any useful crap done."

Trey nodded. "Yeah, I agree. Aunt Charlyce got all the details of the payments and shit worked out, but you and me have got to agree on how to work it with the boys. The thing is, the boys are all from Los Angeles. This is our home. Not one of them wants to spend all their time in a new city.

"Fair enough. Got any ideas?"

"I was kind of stumped, but Royce had some sweet ideas."

"He did?"

James hadn't even considering asking the DI for advice.

"Yeah," Trey replied. "I figure it's not like the military always works their people nine-to-five. So I asked him for suggestions. He talked about using a rotating schedule with a small number of guys." Trey shrugged. "I figure we arrange the boys into teams. It's how we've been training them anyway. We can use teams of six that are set up, so we have three of them in Vegas for three days a week to help start clearing it out. The other half of the team in LA. They get a day off, and then the next week we swap to a new team, so it'll be a few weeks before someone has to work a weird-ass schedule and only have a day off. It'll also keep most of the boys concentrated in LA, so they don't feel like we pulled some bait-and-switch shit on them."

"Sounds good," James offered.

Trey frowned. "Only one last thing to worry about."

"What?"

"What about Lachlan? Not sure if we should have him working this kind of schedule, even if his week won't come up that often."

James grunted. "If he's gonna be part of the team, then he needs to do the same shit as everyone else. Otherwise, it won't work, and he'll become more of a pain in the ass."

Trey chuckled. "Yeah, you're right. I'm being a dumbass. I'm planning to be on the first team, and I'll take him with me unless Royce needs him for training those three days. He can keep an eye on his sorry ass then." He grinned. "Don't worry. I've got this, boss."

"I trust you, Trey. You know that by now, right?"

"Shit, James, you're one of the few people who ever has. I better get talking to the boys about the plan." He hopped out of his seat and headed toward the door, his suit immaculate as always.

I look like a bum, but Trey looks like a professional. Funny how that shit works.

Trey opened the door and stepped out of the room.

James followed up his meeting by clicking around on a few barbeque news sites. High-level bounties had been scarce the last few days. Apparently, a lot of criminals liked to take a vacation at the beginning of the summer, too.

Fifteen minutes later and right in the middle of reading an article entitled "Carolinas Divided: A Sauce Controversy," James' phone buzzed with a text from Sergeant Mack.

Brownstone, you need to come down to the precinct. Lieutenant Hall wants to talk with you.

"What the fuck now?" the bounty hunter grumbled. Why wouldn't that AET cop leave his ass alone?

His phone buzzed again.

No, you aren't being brought in or arrested. Come ASAP.

James sat on a chair in the featureless white-walled interrogation room wondering what the hell was going on. He wasn't going to fight the cops if they planned to arrest him. That might make the next couple of days unpleasant.

I don't have time for this shit. I wasn't even in town for the last big showdown, so it's not like they can bitch at me for blowing shit up.

The door opened, and Sergeant Mack stepped through, a cup of coffee and a donut in hand. He walked over to the table and set them in front of James.

"Just waiting on Lieutenant Hall," the sergeant explained.

"And you're sure I'm not under arrest?"

Mack shrugged. "To be honest, I don't know what the hell is going on. Just that she specifically wanted you to come in. AET asked me to reach out to you since I've worked with you for years and I used to be your landlord.

They wanted this to be, in Hall's words, 'non-confrontational.'"

Did they use Mack to trap me? If they did, he wasn't in on it. No fucking way.

James grabbed the chocolate sprinkled donut and took a bite. Might as well handle another errand while he was at the station.

"Hey, I meant to call you about this shit, Mack, but I need your help with something else. Nothing to do with cops or bounty hunting."

The sergeant took a seat in one of the hard plastic chairs across from James. "What did you need?"

"I was wondering if you'd co-captain a barbeque team."

Mack's interest was piqued. "A barbeque team? Whose?"

"The Brownstone Agency's. We're gonna be doing competitions. Team-building shit, and why pass up a chance to barbeque? We'll have a bunch of smaller groups under the main team, but I'm still looking for someone to help guide the whole crew. Someone who knows their way around a grill."

"A bunch of reformed gangbangers and a bounty hunter? I guess with one cop thrown in the sauces would be pretty fucking wonderful." Mack chuckled. "Maybe that's what our team name could be. PFW. Have to clean it up in case anyone asks. Pretty, fantastic and wonderful."

James shrugged. "I'm always into truth in marketing. 'Fucking' would have to stay in. If people can't handle that, then fuck *them*."

Mack laughed. "You're the captain, and they're your guys."

The door creaked, and Lieutenant Hall stepped in, for once lacking the scowl that always seemed attached to her face whenever she was forced to be near James.

She nodded at the open door. "Sergeant, I'd like to talk to Brownstone alone. This is an AET matter, nothing to do with general police business or bounty hunting."

Mack looked at James, and the bounty hunter nodded back. He doubted Hall would assassinate him in the middle of a police station in a room with a security camera.

The sergeant made his way to the door. "Talk later about PFW?"

"Yeah."

The cop stepped out of the room and closed the door behind him.

Lieutenant Hall didn't sit. She stared at James with her lips pursed, like he was a naughty child who had annoyed her.

James shrugged. "You wanted me, so I'm here."

"Yeah, that you are."

"Before we get into whatever this shit is about, I wanted to congratulate you. Nice job on taking down that witch, by the way. I saw some of the action on the news. She would have fucked me up if I had to take her on."

Maria's brow furrowed as if she were confused by the compliment. She dropped into a chair and folded her hands in front of her. "I guess I'll take that as a compliment on behalf of the guys of the force."

"You're the main tactical team leader. It's a compliment for you, too. I'm a shitty leader, so I give respect to those who aren't."

The lieutenant sighed. "Let's be real, Brownstone. I've

made no secret of the fact I don't like you. Hell, I think I downright hate you."

James grinned. "Yeah. I kind of noticed."

"But I've also been told by the higher-ups that I need to stop blaming you for everything, and…" The lieutenant looked away. "Look, one of the reasons I have problems with you is because of how fucking destructive you are. I joined AET because I didn't like the idea of overpowered people doing whatever the fuck they want. I don't give a shit if magic is back. The strong should protect the weak."

James grunted. "I do my best to keep that shit away from innocent people. Why do you think I came to the cops when all those hitmen were after me? But I'm not gonna fucking cry if some asshole thugs' buildings get busted up. Fuck the Harriken. They got everything they had coming."

"Not saying they didn't." The lieutenant took a deep breath. "When we took down that demon witch, we tore up a lot of cars in the area. We'd gone out of our way to make sure civilians weren't around, were geared up, and ready, and the collateral damage was *still* high."

"Shit happens." James shrugged.

"Yeah, I know. All this crap recently, including the witch and AET's last big battle, has given me a new perspective on what it means to deal with high-level targets."

"A new perspective?"

The cop shrugged. She reached across the table and snatched James' coffee cup. He didn't bother to complain.

She took a sip, eyeing him as if daring him to complain.

"Not saying mass destruction is acceptable, but I accept now that we can't always make the other side take it easy on innocent bystanders. That crazy bitch murdered a bunch of people at that farmer's market for shits and giggles, and she would have killed dozens more if we hadn't stopped her."

James nodded. "Sometimes a hard take-down is just that. I like it when the assholes are hiding in the middle of nowhere, so no one has to get hurt. Dealt with a necromancer in Mexico like that. I could really let loose without any worries."

Lieutenant Hall gulped down more coffee. "Yeah. My first real takedown was a level four hiding at a new construction site. It was fucking annoying as hell because the guy could move shit without touching it, so there was a bunch of dodging wood and steel beams, but it was also easy to keep people away from the scene, and there wasn't much to blow up." She let out a soft chuckle. "It's crazy. When I joined the force, if someone had walked in and talked about magic, we would have sent them to the psych hospital, and now I have a job where I have to worry about fucking magical killers."

"You religious at all, Lieutenant?"

"Huh? Why do you ask?"

James shrugged. "I'm Catholic. I'm a shitty Catholic, but I still try to go to church. Was just thinking about something my priest told me a while back. He was saying how with all this magic coming back that it should remind people that miracles are a real thing. Good magic, not just the bad magic."

"You believe that, Brownstone? It's hard sometimes not

to believe the Man Downstairs isn't the guy winning the long game."

The bounty hunter grunted and shook his head. "Every time you take down an asshole like that witch, you save people. Shit is fucked-up all over right now, but it's only been twenty years since magic came back in full. We'll probably figure out this sooner rather than later, and our grandkids won't get why magic was even a big deal."

Lieutenant Hall set down the coffee cup and snickered. "I'm surprised. You didn't strike me as the optimistic sort, Brownstone."

"I don't know *what* I am, but I've got people I give a shit about. All I can do is beat down the assholes who might hurt them."

She looked uncomfortable for a moment. "Okay, anyway, I didn't call you here to trade takedown stories."

"Why did you call me here, Lieutenant?"

She locked eyes with him. "We had another big takedown right before the witch. She didn't have an official bounty, but she would have easily been a level five."

James kept his face impassive. In truth, he felt bad about setting up the AET. He'd not expected the fake Shay to be so tough, and the last thing he'd ever wanted was for a cop to get hurt; even cops who hated him. They were all on the same side in the end.

"The woman you asked me about," he offered.

"Yeah. New evidence has come up. We're not so sure she was even human."

"Huh, really? Guess that would explain why she gave you so much trouble."

"We think she was a disguised Oriceran, a type of elf

called a Drow. We also believe she was linked to a string of murders around the same period. Some information suggests she's got three buddies in town. Not a hundred percent certain, but there are three weirdos with powerful magic who have been asking around about you. Considering what happened before, I'm betting these three weirdos are Drow in disguise."

The lieutenant watched him for a moment, scrutinizing his face for any sign of recognition.

That's who the fake Shay was, a Drow? And three more are here. Damn it. Are they looking for Alison? I don't know shit about these Drow, but her mom ran away from them, and if they'd try to kill a bunch of cops and murder people, I don't want her anywhere near those fuckers.

If they are anywhere near as tough as Alison's mom, this might be a fucking problem. I've got to take care of these assholes before she comes back home and gets caught in the crossfire.

I promised Nicole I'd protect Alison, and she's my daughter now. Fuck anyone who comes after her. I'll kick their asses all the way into the World in Between.

James shrugged, blank-faced. "What's this got to do with me? I really had no idea who that woman was. You used your artifact, remember? It proved I was telling the truth."

"Yeah, I know."

"Anyway, I'm a bounty hunter, not a cop. If they don't attack me, there won't be an issue. From what it sounds like, they don't have a bounty, so it's not worth my time to go fucking with them."

Lieutenant Hall chuckled. "I had a conversation the

other day with a couple of homicide detectives in Las Vegas, West and Lafayette."

James frowned. "What's that have to do with anything?"

"I knew you'd worked with them during your little Vegas escapade, so I wanted to get the truth from the horse's mouth. You're not the King of Vegas like you are Los Angeles, so I figured if you were a piece of shit they'd let me know."

James grunted but didn't say anything.

Lieutenant Hall leaned forward, a smirk on her face. "They told me all sorts of shit, a lot of it off the record, mostly how you were obsessed with a promise to a little girl, how you didn't really give a shit about the money as long as you took down the killer, crap like that." She sighed. "This is a problem, Brownstone. Don't you see?"

"Not following you."

"I thought I had you figured out. Thought you were just a thug who got off on beating people down and got away with it because you were smart enough to beat down mostly other thugs, but now I see it's bullshit."

"You don't know shit about me, Lieutenant."

She sat back up. "Sure, but I do know you're in the process of adopting a girl whose parents died, and she's off at some boarding school. Maybe you were a thug before, and your priest's sermon finally got to you. Maybe you had a birthday and started thinking there is something more to life than being a piece of shit. All I know is I'm fucking annoyed because I have to think of you as an actual human being."

James snorted. *If only you knew, Lieutenant. If only you knew.*

She held up a hand. "Look, I don't know all the bullshit you're into, Brownstone, and I know you've pulled some crap that should probably get you locked up. But that doesn't change the fact that these three Drow are sniffing around for you, and it'll only be a matter of time before they come at you. Since you're not hiding in a safehouse, I'm guessing they're trying to scope out your capabilities before they hit you. And when these assholes come chasing you, AET wants a piece of their ass."

James stared at the AET lieutenant, his mouth agape. "You want to help me?"

"Serve and protect. That's what cops do." Lieutenant Hall stood. "Or this might be an 'enemy of my enemy is my friend' deal. I've been told the Drow are about the worst assholes you can have messing around, and I don't need an infestation in my town. We've got plenty of weird assholes here already."

Drow are that *bad of news? I wonder if Alison knew all this already, but she's safe at the school. If I take all these three assholes out, she'll be safe for the summer.*

Maria headed toward the door but stopped a few feet from it. "Given the shit I saw the last time we took down a Drow, we can't risk them going after you in the city. You have to run, Brownstone, draw them away from a crowded area, and we can help."

"You're really gonna risk your life to help me?"

"Yeah. I don't care where you take them. I just don't want this shit going down in some park." Lieutenant Hall fished a business card out of her pocket and tossed on the table. "Keep in touch, and AET will have your back." She stepped into the hallway.

James stared at the open interrogation room door. After all this time, AET wanted to help him rather than take him down.

Maybe it's a trick. Maybe she's just trying to get me somewhere she can finish me off, but fuck, even with the amulet I might need the help against three Drow.

I've got to take the chance. I need to take these assholes down for Alison.

18

"Is that an acceptable starting date, Detective?" Charlyce inquired.

"Yes, we should have all the financial paperwork done on our end before then," Detective West replied over the speakerphone. "Once your first team is here, we'll arrange a meeting so they can meet everyone they'll be dealing with at the department."

Trey sat beside his aunt, his arms crossed, letting her do her thing. He smiled. She'd gone from homeless vagrant to negotiating with cops for professional services in a matter of weeks.

"Excellent," Charlyce replied in a crisp voice. "Now, I just want to be very clear on this matter, and the contracts and paperwork we've sent in reflect this as well. You're hiring the Brownstone Agency, not James Brownstone. Not saying he'll never show up, but he won't be part of any of the rotating teams. Mr. Brownstone concentrates almost entirely on level four and above bounties."

"Understood, Ms. Garfield. Fortunately, we don't have as many high-level whackos running around Vegas as you do in Los Angeles. We appreciate and understand the limits of what you're offering, and we're more than happy with it. This will still be a great help to the department."

"Is there anything else you wanted to discuss, Detective?"

"That should be enough for now. Just have Trey give us a call when the first team arrives."

"I will," Trey offered.

"Talk to you soon." Detective West hung up.

Trey clapped his hands together. "We're really moving up in the world for an ex-gang leader and his homeless aunt."

She laughed. "Oh, Trey."

"Still need to find a small office up there. The big man's made sure we'll have the cash, but he's not gonna be the one to pick it out."

Charlyce nodded at her phone. "I've already narrowed it down with some searches online."

"Then the only thing left is to run up to Vegas. Me, you, three of the boys. Everything should be okay down here in the meantime. Royce says he'll keep an eye on Lachlan."

Trey's aunt let out a small chuckle.

"What's so funny?"

"It's like you said, Trey. A month ago, I was more concerned about my next meal than contracts. We're respectable folk now, helping stop criminals. I just…" She wiped away a happy tear. "It's a dream come true."

Trey pushed away from the table and stood. "Yeah, couldn't say I expected any of this shit. Whew." He rubbed the back of his neck. "But we ain't finished yet. I'll text the big man and let him know we're heading to Vegas. If any bullshit happens with the rest of the boys, I can be back here in hours to knock some heads."

Charlyce looked at her nephew with concern. "Are you worried?"

Trey laughed. "Nah. I'd like to see any of those dumb-asses try to take on a Marine and not get their asses handed to them."

James stepped into the Leanan Sídhe. Happy chatter from the crowd filled the room, but unlike his arrival at the Black Sun the other morning, no one cheered. People glanced at the door to offer him a polite nod. Here he was still just another regular and not James Brownstone, famous bounty hunter and Scourge of Harriken.

The Professor sat gulping down thick amber liquid at a table in back, rosy-cheeked. He waved at James.

The bounty hunter didn't head straight to the back. He marched over to a chalkboard hanging above the bar where contestants could sign up for the latest Bard of Filth competition, pulled a piece of chalk off the holder, and scribbled his name on the board.

Silence rippled from the bar. Someone even turned the TV off. Dozens of people stared at James and the chalkboard.

"James Brownstone has just signed up for next week's official Bard of Filth competition," the bartender shouted.

"We're going to hear dirty limericks or a dirty song from James Brownstone!"

Wild cheers and clapping followed.

Oh, fuck my life.

James groaned. He shook his head and walked toward the Professor, several people patting him on the back as he passed.

"You'll kick ass, Brownstone," one man shouted.

"Make it extra-filthy," a woman commented.

James arrived at the Professor's table and took a seat. The Professor stared at him, eyes narrowed as if he suspected the bounty hunter was a Drow in disguise.

A passing waitress headed over to the table. "Can I get you anything, Mr. Brownstone?"

"An Irish Stout please," James rumbled.

"No problem." She smiled and hurried to the bar, her movement through the crowd a thing of surprising grace and caution.

The Professor picked up his glass and took another sip of beer. "I never thought I'd see the day you'd sign up voluntarily. I was planning to force you my own way."

James grunted. "I wasn't ready before. I'm ready now."

"Are you now, lad? Then give me an example. Prove to me you won't embarrass us both."

James cleared his throat.

"There once was a man they called James,
Who loved meat cooked with open flames,
His house got burned down,
Which gave him a frown,
So he kicked ass without taking names."

The Professor rubbed his chin and nodded approvingly.

"Not bad. Good flow, but that's more threatening than filthy. Show me you can truly aspire to be the Bard of Filth. I want *depravity*, not wrath."

"There once was a man they called Brock,
Who worked like a bitch 'round the clock,
A vacation he earned,
For the lessons he'd learned,
Like fucking your mom with his cock."

The Professor burst out laughing and clapped. "Okay, lad. I'm not sure what Oriceran magic you used to go from pathetic loser to saucy and filthy, but that was pretty damned good. You might not win the competition, but at least now I know you can put up a fight."

James snorted. "You actually *liked* that shit?"

"Aye, James. The first one was okay, but the second one proves you understand what a good filthy limerick is all about." He grinned. "I'm finally looking forward to this competition."

The waitress returned with James' beer and set it in front of him before departing with a smile.

The Professor waited for her to retreat into the crowd. "But filthy limericks aren't why you're here today. I've got a job for you, lad."

"A bounty?"

He shook his head. "More of a courier thing. Kind of like Seattle."

James grunted. "Isn't this more of a Shay job?"

"Aye, but she's not available, so I'm having to go to junior varsity in this case." The Professor chuckled. "More seriously, this particular artifact is dangerous enough that it would benefit from your unique skill in beating the living snot out of anyone who might come after you. We need to get this artifact out of anyone else's hands. It's too powerful for *anyone* to have it. Too much a temptation."

"But if you send me after it, *I'll* have it."

"Aye, but out of all the bad choices, you're the least bad in my opinion. Once you deliver it, I can stick it somewhere where even *I* won't be able to get to it."

James picked up his beer and downed some of it, enjoying the roasted and bitter undertones. "Why not just destroy it if it's so dangerous?"

"Because we'd need the equivalent of a Mount Doom worth of magic to destroy it. No single person has that much, so it's easier to just hide the artifact."

James shrugged and took another drink. "You're the expert. I'll focus on the part that involves ass-kicking. What is it, where is it, and who else wants it?"

"It's in Arizona. I'll send you the address once you're on the road. This matter is sensitive enough that even *I'm* paranoid about it. As for the cost, I've paid half up front."

"How much will I need to bring with me for the other half?"

"Oh, don't worry about it. You'll find out when you get there."

James frowned. "But if it's a—"

The Professor cut him off with a raised hand. "It'll be fine. I don't even want to describe the item on the off chance anyone is listening. You'll go to the address, and you'll ask for the item being held for a Jake Greystone. I've already made a deposit."

"Jake Greystone?"

The Professor smirked. "Aye."

"Very funny."

"I thought so."

James frowned. "If it's so dangerous should I fly to pick it up and bring it back? Or is it another one of those exploding if it gets too high kind of deals?"

"I honestly don't know, but I wouldn't advise it. It's been known to disrupt technology in the past. I'll be providing you with a lead box that has been enchanted with various runes."

"And that shit will keep me safe?"

The Professor polished off his beer, slammed the glass on the table, and shrugged. "Maybe. I'd hope so."

"Maybe?"

"Very few things are certain in life, lad. Not even death and taxes anymore." The Professor wiped his mouth with his sleeve. "Unlike my last little courier job for you, I don't actually expect any trouble this time. This should be a simple pickup if you're lucky."

"That's a big if."

Shit. Better stop by the warehouse to grab my amulet.

Shay's eyes fluttered open when her phone rang, and she turned her head to check who it was.

"James?" She lifted it from the nightstand. "Something wrong?"

James grunted. "What, can't I call you? The last text you sent me said it'd be okay to call you."

"No, no, it's fine. Just didn't expect it." Shay shrugged,

even though he couldn't see it. "Seriously, though, everything okay with you?"

"Yeah. Just running to Arizona on a little errand for the Professor. No big deal."

"No big deal? If the Professor wanted *you* as a courier, it's a big deal."

James chuckled. "Things have been quiet. No problems over here."

"If you say so."

Shay narrowed her eyes. Something about the tone felt forced to her, as if he were trying to hide something.

Fuck. Am I just being paranoid because of that video thing?

Confronting him over the hacker matter wouldn't help. If he'd avoided using Peyton, James had a reason, and she either needed to trust him or push him away.

Don't think I'll let him know Peyton filled me in on that bar shit even if he couldn't find the video. I shouldn't have ratted him out to James to begin with. It was a bitch move.

"There's a sweet barbeque place in Arizona I'll finally be able to check out," James explained.

"Probably secretly the last base of the Harriken."

"Fuck, I don't care. If there are any Harriken left and they make good barbeque, they deserve to live."

Shay laughed and rolled onto her side on the bed. "That's all criminals need to do to survive? Cook good barbeque?"

"It's a start."

"So in five years they'll be no gangs or mobsters, just barbeque restaurants everywhere?"

"Sounds a lot like heaven."

"What about for the vegetarians?"

James chuckled. "They'll just have to convert. Hold on a sec." Scratching filled the line for a moment. "Need to grab some gas soon. Gonna need to let you go."

"No problem. Talk to you later. And…"

"Yeah?"

"I love you, James."

"I love you, too, Shay."

Shay sighed and ended the call. She fell onto her back and wiped away the tears that were leaking out.

She loved James, but she didn't trust him, even though she was one who'd lived a lie her entire life and still lied to him every time they talked. She convinced herself not telling him about Project Nephilim and Project Ragnarok was for his own good, but after spending half her life deceiving others, she couldn't discount that being truthful would forever elude her.

"My man is an alien who grew up having trouble understanding how to relate to people. Fuck. He's not me. He's lived a painfully straightforward life, even if he hid his amulet. If I can't learn to trust *him*, who the hell am I going to trust?"

I'll do better, James. I'm working on it. It's just gonna take a while.

19

Reyal looked into the mirror. She didn't like the false face she'd generated with her magic. At least she enjoyed the black color of their *borrowed* Porsche. Her knowledge of Earth vehicle aesthetics was limited, but from what she could tell her taste in the matter signaled refinement even among humans.

Zavan frowned. "Why are we going this way? Is this west or east?"

"I believe it's east." Reyal turned at an intersection, frowning.

Her leader frowned and shook his head. "No, we're heading west judging by the sun. Why are we are going in the wrong direction?"

"The Skill Ring helps me drive, not navigate, Zavan. Do you expect me to have memorized the layout of the roads in the human city? Why not use an active tracking spell?"

Kaella chuckled in the back.

Zavan lifted his hand to conjure another tracking spell

but stopped and shook his head. "The more magic we use, the greater the chance our enemies—whether from the consulate or elsewhere—might home in on us. If we're captured, it'll make things difficult for the queen or force us into unnecessary confrontations."

"I don't fear confrontation," Reyal objected.

"This is not our world, and we're not here to kill weaklings. We're here to find the princess. If we're too obvious, Brownstone will realize we're coming for her. He might move her into the heart of some Light Elf enclave or something equally annoying." Zavan shook his head. "No, we must be cautious—not out of safety but because our mission demands it. Now get us heading east."

"Fine," Reyal muttered. "Then don't complain if I get lost on occasion."

"Go in the right direction, and we'll find him. The farther we move from the city, the easier it'll be for us to confront him without interference." Zavan looked out the window as a car passed him. "Soon we will force Brownstone to tell us where the princess is. Then we can leave this wretched planet and punish Brownstone for ever daring to interfere with the Drow."

What the fuck? This is the right address, but this can't be the place.

The door above the bell jingled as James stepped into Lake Treasures Pawn Shop. Dingy metal shelves filled with a variety of goods lined the cramped room, and a bored-looking woman with an unruly mop of brown hair sat behind a glass window. The window broke up the gate that otherwise blocked off the back half of the store. The bottom of the window was set atop a folding panel.

Several pistols and rifles hung on the wall in the back. A long, thin red wooden wand hung near the far end of the wall.

It couldn't be an actual wand, could it? Shit, I don't know how that works anyway.

The clerk's jaw worked a thick wad of bubblegum as she stared at her phone. Other than a quick glance upon James' entry, she hadn't bothered to look his way or acknowledge his existence.

James walked over to the window. The woman continued looking at her phone until the bounty hunter cleared his throat.

The clerk tapped the phone and set it on the counter. "You ever watch *The Real Dwarf Mafia of New York?*"

James shook his head. "I only watch cooking shows."

"I just started watching it. It's a reality show. They follow these dwarf guys around New York. They never say they are mobsters, but they sure are talking about some shady shit. My cousin Sheila says it's all fake, but I'm like, how could it be fake? I mean, these dwarves would curse the guys if they were making shit up."

"Who knows? Got plenty of other mafias in New York. Why not add one more?"

The clerk grinned and blew a bubble. It popped, and she slurped the gum back in. "What can I do you for, hon?"

James didn't like lying to random people, but the Professor had a plan, and giving a fake name was a key part.

"My name is Jake Greystone. I'm here to pick up something."

"Oh, yeah. Wondering when you would show up. Just need you to pay the rest."

James frowned. The woman expected him, but he had a hard time wrapping his mind around the idea that such a dangerous magical object would be in some seedy Lake Havasu City pawn shop.

He pulled his phone out of his pocket, ready to make an electronic transfer. "How much?"

"Fifty."

Shit. Fifty thousand? This is why the fucking Professor should have told me how much it'd be.

The clerk popped her gum again. "Hey, hon, you would be doing me a real favor if you wouldn't pay using a fifty-dollar bill. Need some change. Five tens would be great."

"Five tens?" James blinked.

Not fifty thousand dollars. Fifty dollars. So not only was he picking up a dangerous magical object from a pawn shop, but he was doing it for fifty dollars. Even counting the Professor's deposit, that made a grand total of a hundred dollars.

James put his phone back in his pocket and pulled out his wallet. "Sorry. I've got two twenties and a ten."

"Hey, better than nothing." The woman opened the panel at the bottom of the window.

James slid the bills over to her.

"One sec, hon." She closed the panel and disappeared into the back room. A minute later she returned, a small ceramic figurine of a crying clown in hand. She passed it under the window.

"Here you go, Jake. Glad you got your clown back. Family heirloom?"

James grunted. "Yeah, some shit like that." He picked up the figurine and shook his head. "Weird."

"Huh?"

"Nothing. Was just thinking about something else." James gave the woman a nod and made his way out of the store, the bell jingling again.

The nigh-indestructible super magic item was an ugly-ass clown figurine. It didn't feel warm to the touch, glow, or move on its own. Some wizard had a good sense of humor.

James threw open the passenger door and opened the glyph-covered lead box. He tossed the figurine inside and closed the box before making his way around to the driver's seat.

He slipped the key into the ignition. "Hope this shit works. Otherwise, it's a long way back to LA."

The engine turned over without trouble; no strange pulses, no demons, no fireballs blasting out of portals.

"Nice," James mumbled to himself. "For once, shit is going all right."

He pulled the truck out of the parking lot and onto the road. The lack of a pitched battle with a pissed-off wizard meant he had plenty of time to hit up a barbeque place.

Nice to have a trip that doesn't end with shit blowing up.

Maria's desk phone rang. She stopped her work on the

budget increase form she'd been filling out to pick up the phone.

"Lieutenant Hall, AET."

"Lieutenant," answered a receptionist over the phone. "There's a call for you from the Oriceran Consulate. It's the consul."

"Put him right through."

The line clicked.

"Hello?"

Someone cleared their throat on the other end. "Good afternoon, Lieutenant. We didn't get a chance to talk directly when you spoke with my staff previously."

"That's okay. The information he provided on the Drow was useful in verifying some of my concerns."

"Yes, about the Drow…"

Maria frowned. "What about them?"

"It's come to my attention that there was previously Drow activity in this area. I apologize for this not being made clearer. Some of the staff aren't always the most diligent when it comes to our records."

Yeah, right. Just because I'm not magical doesn't mean I'll fall for that bullshit lie, asshole.

"No big deal. I'm less concerned with past Drow visits than current ones."

The silence stretched so long Maria thought she'd been disconnected. "Hello? You still there?"

The consul sighed on the other end. "Because of the concerns you raised, I've been having my people pay closer attention to unusual magic in the greater Los Angeles area. They've been able to confirm there are three Drow in the county. Although it's difficult to track them, they are currently heading east toward the Inland Empire at a high rate of speed."

You fuckers have known all along, haven't you? Finally decided to play nice? Maybe figured you couldn't handle it?

She kept her voice level when she spoke. "Can you track them specifically, like give me coordinates or something like that, so I can task a drone?"

"No, I'm sorry, Lieutenant. It was mere fortune that we have been able to track them at all. I strongly suspect they're trying to keep a low magical profile."

"Any description of the Drow or their vehicle?"

"I'm sorry. That information isn't available at this time. I'd pass it along if I had it."

Would he? "Okay, thanks anyway. Let me know if you hear anything else."

"Of course. Goodbye, Lieutenant Hall." The consul hung up.

Maria stood and tried to decide her next move. The Drow were leaving her jurisdiction, but she had no idea where they were going. She couldn't put out an APB or call the highway patrol on three unidentified suspects in an unidentified vehicle, but if she let one Drow in, there went the neighborhood.

Or the entire West Coast.

"Why are they going east? Wait, where the fuck is Brownstone right now?"

2 0

James relaxed at a table on the patio and munched down on pulled pork. The lead box with the Clown of Doom sat next to him, but the delicious savory flavors of the meat and sauce in his mouth killed any lingering worries about the artifact.

He'd never been to Rebel BBQ, but he enjoyed a place that had a smoker right out front. It proved their confidence. They weren't hiding anything from anyone.

Almost every table was filled with people smiling and enjoying their barbeque. Another good sign of quality.

James swallowed another bite and chuckled.

Shit. Someday I could see myself running a place like this. No fucking Clown of Doom or body-jumping necromancers or Drow, except Alison.

What would Shay say to that? Probably, "You can't run a restaurant, dumbass."

A couple next to him noticed his stupid grin, grabbed their food, and moved inside.

Some people just couldn't handle a happy man.

The Porsche screamed down the highway, Reyal's hands tight around the wheel. Zavan's risk of another tracking spell might have alerted someone, but it was worth it.

She whipped around several cars. Their suppression spell should keep police attention off the vehicle as long as they drove by them fast enough. This was one of the few times she'd found technology helpful for magic. It'd also protect against scrying and most tracking spells as long as they kept moving fast.

Their previous directional woes were a minor concern. The important thing was that Brownstone was still far away from Los Angeles and whatever allies he had gathered there. His trip out of the city had decided his cruel fate.

We're coming, James Brownstone. Prepare to face the full might of the Drow.

The sultry podcaster's voice drifted from the F-350's speaker. "Men and women might be different, but it's important to realize those differences aren't a matter of superiority or inferiority. They are complementary, not competitive. A perfect couple is a harmony of the masculine and the feminine in both parties."

Huh. Both Shay and I do like to kick a lot of ass. Is that masculine? We're both protective. Isn't that kind of more a mothering thing? So is it feminine? Fuck if I know.

The podcast cut out as his text alert chimed. He'd been expecting one from Shay since he'd already sent off a text to her explaining how he was already on his way back home and there had been no trouble. The text wasn't from his girlfriend, but rather another woman he had a difficult relationship with.

Lieutenant Hall.

Call me ASAP, Brownstone.

It was still hard to wrap his mind around working with a woman who'd hated his guts and probably wanted to kill him until recently, but he wasn't going to turn down backup. Especially AET backup.

James dialed her number, and she answered on the first ring.

"Where are you at this exact moment, Brownstone?"

"I-10E on my way back to LA from Arizona, but I'm several hours away. I had some shit to do in Lake Havasu City. Why?"

"Fuck. You're too damned far away." She sounded almost concerned for him.

"What's going on?"

"Got Drow heading east out of LA. I think they're finally making their move."

James grunted. That was what he got for thinking the job would be easy. "How many?"

"Best I can tell, three. Let me tell you, Brownstone, these are serious bastards. Just one of them came close to taking out my entire team, and we were geared up and ready. These are three nuclear bombs we can't have going off anywhere near civilians. Agreed?"

One hand tightened around the wheel. The other went to his chest. The amulet rested under his shirt, still separated from his skin by a metal divider. At least he had a chance to win with it.

Guess we're gonna see if a space alien is worth three magical aliens.

"Agreed," James replied, his voice deeper and more grinding than normal. "You think they are tracking me directly, or just heading my way?"

"Don't know, but I'm going to assume they are tracking you directly."

"Good."

"Good?"

"Yeah," James offered. "That means I can lead them somewhere real deserted." He furrowed his brow. "How about I head toward the Salton Sea?"

"That's a good choice. I remember when that place was still worth the name. These days it's mostly empty of people and water. You do what you need to do. I'm going to pull some strings and scramble to catch up. If those Drow are after you, at least you could fight out there without a bunch of civilians getting hurt."

James took a deep breath. "You said you'll catch up?"

"Yeah. AET doesn't have long-range aircraft. Have to figure something out."

"But you are planning to *help*?"

Maria snorted. "Yeah. We've had our differences, but that doesn't mean I want some assholes from Oriceran killing you. Like I said at the station, my eyes have been opened lately. I'm not saying we're going to be best friends, Brownstone, but we should at least try to work better together."

"Fair enough. But what happens if the Drow don't show up?"

"I doubt we'll get that lucky."

"Maybe. But I've got shit to do. I can't sit in the middle of nowhere all damned night."

Maria laughed. "Suck it up, Brownstone. I'll have my guys bring some marshmallows that you can have if you don't die."

Trey, Shorty, Max, and Kevin all sat around the police conference table in black suits. Trey, Shorty, and Max looked relaxed, but Kevin kept tugging at his collar.

"I can't believe we have to wear this shit. Yo, man, I told you I didn't want to wear no suit."

Trey snorted. "I'd beat your ass, but we're in a police station. We're not representing some punk-ass street gang no more. We're representing the Brownstone Agency. These are official colors, bitch. This, or navy blue. Get used to it."

Charlyce cleared her throat. "Trey, you don't need to talk to him like that."

He scrubbed a hand over his face and took a deep breath. His aunt was right. It was time to become Smooth Trey for the cops.

Detectives West and Lafayette filtered into the room. They headed over to Trey to shake his hand, and then made their way down the line to the other men.

"Pleasure to meet you and your men, Mr. Garfield."

"Likewise, Detective." Trey pointed to his boys in turn. "Shorty, Max, and Kevin."

Damn, Shorty needs a new nickname. Wonder if they are gonna take us seriously with a guy named Shorty.

The cops finished shaking hands and moved over to the front of the table. "We're handling this for now because it was our idea, but in the future, we won't be your main contacts because we're homicide detectives. Sergeant Choi in Bounty Processing will be your primary contact. You'll be meeting with him in about twenty minutes. We might work more closely with you in cases where you're going after people wanted in connection with open homicide cases, though."

Trey offered a cool nod even as his heart tried to gallop out of his chest. He'd gotten used to the respect of Sergeant Mack, but he'd had contact with the man even before the Brownstone Agency. These two detectives in a new city were giving their respect without knowing anything other than that Trey and the boys were bounty hunters.

Shit, I have really done it. Trey the gang leader is gone.

Shorty set down the rib he'd chomped on his plate and blinked several times. "Damn, Brownstone's always going on and on about this Jessie Rae's, but I thought it was just bullshit, but this…damn. I think I should marry this sauce and have little sauce babies."

Trey laughed. "That's why they call it God Sauce. Why do you think my big man is always is coming here, Shorty?"

The men and Aunt Charlyce all clustered around two tables in the small dining room, enjoying several pounds of ribs and pulled pork as part of their celebratory early dinner. After their meeting at the police station, they'd found a small office unit with a loft living space attached. It'd be the perfect headquarters for the small visiting Las Vegas teams. If they started bringing in more people in the future, they could figure out something else. At least they'd already be established.

"That was crazy, yo," Kevin commented after polishing off the last bite of his first pulled pork sandwich. "I kept expecting those 5-0 to try and bust our asses, not show us all that respect."

Shorty and Max nodded their agreement.

Trey shrugged. "That's what I've been trying to tell y'all. Things are different now. We're on Team Brownstone. We stay with him, and we show our respect. The cops will show their respect back, especially when we bring down these nasty-ass criminals with bounties."

"You say it like it ain't no big deal, Trey," Kevin responded. "But I ain't never had a cop be so polite to me."

"Give respect, you get respect. That's what Mr. Brownstone does, and that's what we're gonna do."

The owner of Jessie Rae's, Michael, stepped out from the back and headed over to their tables. "Sorry to have eavesdropped, but I couldn't help but overhear a few things." He smiled at Shorty. "And thanks for appreciating the food."

Shorty grinned. "Thanks for making it, man."

Michael returned his attention to Trey. "I didn't realize everyone here worked for James."

Charlyce gave Michael a bright smile. "That's right. We're all part of the Brownstone Agency. James talks this place up so much I had to bring the boys to show them the truth. Hell, I think we're going to be spending a lot of time here in the future."

"Any friends of James Brownstone are friends of mine." Michael glanced at a photo showing him and James at a barbeque competition. "And going forward, any employee of the Brownstone Agency will get a ten percent discount."

Aunt Charlyce clapped her hands together. "Oh, that is so generous of you." She picked up her phone and started tapping away at it, her brow furrowed.

"Small price to pay. I'm sure by the time you guys are done, there won't be any crime left in Vegas."

Everyone laughed, and a huge grin split Trey's face.

Look out, Las Vegas. Trey Garfield and his boys are here.

Forty-five minutes later, most of the boys had eaten their fill. All except Shorty. Michael was more than happy to keep serving him. Everyone else had fallen into light chatter about all the cool casinos and resorts they'd hit on their day off, but Aunt Charlyce spent most of the time hunched over her phone.

Her head shot up. "Go over to the register and pay, Trey."

Trey looked her way. "Huh?"

Charlyce shook her head at her nephew. "What do you think I've been doing since I stopped eating?"

"I don't know, looking up local hairdressers?"

She scoffed. "Looking up bounties, you fool. We ain't here as tourists. We got a job to do."

Trey grinned. "Looks like Nana passed a little of her attitude down a generation." He stood and smoothed down his suit jacket. "You heard the woman. Let's show the police just how badass the Brownstone Agency is."

Shorty looked at his latest pile of ribs mournfully. "But my food, man."

Trey rolled his eyes. "Just have Michael put it in a to-go box."

Trey strolled up to the worn and peeling front door, a smile plastered on his face. Shorty and Kevin were watching the back door. Max waited, his arms crossed, in front of Trey's truck. Aunt Charlyce wasn't there, having taken the opportunity to check around and bring some food to some of her old homeless friends. One of them had actually given her a tip that had helped lead the team to the house.

Let's see how this shit goes. This is their first real job.

Trey knocked on the door and waited.

The sound of a deadbolt sliding followed, and then the bottom lock clicking open.

A portly man in a wifebeater cracked the door open, a chain still attached on top. "Who the fuck are you? If this is about buying magazines or some shit, I don't want any."

Trey smiled. "Curtis Mayhew?"

"I don't know you, fucker. Get off my property."

"You're a renter, don't get so cocky." Trey scoffed. "Let me make this simple, Mr. Mayhew. I'm Trey Garfield with the Brownstone Agency. We've got your place surrounded, and you're gonna come out here and let me handcuff your ass. Then I'll drag you to the police station. Or you can resist, and I kick the crap out of you, and the same shit happens anyway in the end. Your choice, asshole."

Curtis blinked several times, his mouth open. "Bounty hunters," he screamed.

Trey delivered a spinning back kick to the door. The door burst open, the chain ripping off, and slammed right into Curtis' face. The man hissed in pain and stumbled backward.

The bounty hunter charged the stumbling criminal in front of him. Trey slammed him into a nearby wall, then delivered several quick punches to the man's gut. Curtis collapsed to the ground, groaning, blood pouring down his face from a forehead laceration.

Loud footsteps sounded from the back of the house. Trey gritted his teeth and looked between the downed Curtis and the back of the house.

Shit. Wait. I ain't alone anymore. That's the whole damned point. I've got a team, and I got two boys who can handle the other fool.

Trey dropped to a knee and whipped out his handcuffs to secure the groaning Curtis Mayhew. Once the man was handcuffed, he shot back up and sprinted toward the back. Several loud thuds sounded from the back.

No gunshots. That's good.

He yanked out his pistol and rushed through the open back door. Shorty's knee rested on the back of another man splayed on the ground. The junior bounty hunter was pulling out his handcuffs, and Kevin had his gun trained on the guy.

"A level two and a level one," Trey announced. "Damn. Teams really do make a difference. Let's go drop these fools off with the 5-0."

Trey shot Sergeant Choi a huge grin. The cop looked between him and the two suspects being shoved along by his boys. The cop stared at the battered bounties, pure disbelief etched on his face.

"Level two and level one for processing, Sergeant," Trey announced.

"We didn't talk all that long ago. A few hours."

"Yeah, that's true enough."

The sergeant chuckled and started entering processing data into his computer. "That was damned fast. Don't know if Brownstone himself could bring in two guys that quickly."

Kevin sauntered up and fluffed out his suit jacket. "That's because we are the Brownstone Agency. We get shit done in hours what takes others a week."

Trey crossed his arms and nodded. He thought he'd known pride when he was a gang leader, thought he'd known pride when he'd caught his first bounty. That was *nothing* compared to the pride he felt in his team at that moment.

"Now that you've said that, we'd best be living up to it in the future."

Thundering boots echoed through the nearby hallway in the police station. Sergeant Mack frowned and looked up from his computer.

What the hell?

Sergeant Mack rushed toward the sound. No alarms were going off in the station, and he'd not heard anything about major deployments or incidents requiring a full departmental response. Everyone had been on edge ever since the farmer's market massacre. Occasionally someone called in a false alarm, terrified of the idea a rogue witch of Oriceran releasing the full wrath of their magic.

An armored AET officer turned the corner, his helmet in hand. He slowed for a moment and took a deep breath before preparing to run after the rest of his team.

"Weber," Mack shouted. "What the hell is going on? You got a level four or higher pop up? Please tell me we don't have a copycat attack on a public event."

The AET sergeant stopped. "Nope, but we do have

three presumed hostile level-five equivalents closing on James Brownstone at the Salton Sea."

"What the hell is he doing out there?"

"Luring the bad guys away from anyone who might get hurt."

Mack took a deep breath. "Brownstone can't win against three level fives. Even *he's* not that tough."

Weber nodded. "I know. Lieutenant Hall's lined up some helicopters to get us there to back him up. We've got full deflectors, railguns, rocket drones—the works. Full deployment package. We're going to light those bastards up like we did that witch."

"The AET is going there to help Brownstone?"

"Yeah." Weber smiled. "Things have changed, and it's about damned time. Look, I've got to go. We're wheels-up on the choppers in not that long. If we don't hurry, those level fives will shred him. We're probably cutting it close as it is."

Mack nodded and sighed. "How much room you got on those choppers?"

"Why?"

"Salton Sea's too far away for me to drive and get there in time. I want to hop a ride."

"I don't know, Mack. This is an AET operation. We don't have any spare deflectors."

The other sergeant snorted. "You all are way out of your jurisdiction anyway if you're flying to the Salton Sea. Don't feed me that shit about procedure and rules now, Weber. And it's *my* damned life to risk."

The AET sergeant turned and motioned down the hall. "Follow me, but if Lieutenant Hall tells you to suck it then don't blame me."

The long hours of the California summer meant darkness was still hours away. James didn't know if that would be an advantage. Maybe being a Dark Elf meant that light bothered them, but it didn't seem to bother Alison.

Maybe dark just means evil fucks in this case.

The dried-out lakebed was the perfect symbol of James' life. The Salton Sea had given its all, but evaporation and outside redirection had first reduced it to a salty mess and finally to sediment plains devoid of much in the way of life.

James shook his head. No, he couldn't think that way. He had people who cared about him. Giving up was not an option.

Shit. I can't let it end like this. If I die here, I won't even have said goodbye.

James stepped out of the truck and pulled out his phone. He stared into the distance as the phone rang.

"What's up, James?" Shay answered.

He hesitated for a moment before he finally forced his mouth open. "I just wanted to let you know that no matter what happens to me, I love you."

"Yeah, that doesn't sound ominous as fuck at all. What's going on?"

"Some shit has come up, and I just wanted to make sure I called you before I dealt with it."

"Shit? What shit? Dangerous shit?"

James grunted. "I was wrong about everything being okay. Turns out three Drow are hunting my ass. I'm out at the Salton Sea and LAPD AET is supposed to be backing me up, but I don't know they'll get here in time."

"Why the hell are you at the Salton Sea instead of the middle of LA where you can get cop backup? Or, shit, military backup? Doesn't a bunch of Oricerans showing up to murder random Americans count as an invasion?"

"You saw the aftermath of what Nicole did to those Grayson mercs, and she was just the one Drow. I can't risk people getting hurt. This was a nice place where I knew there wouldn't be a lot of people. Don't know. Maybe I'm wrong. The Drow might not be here to kill me, but everything I've heard makes me think we probably won't be swapping barbeque recipes."

"This is bullshit, James. Complete fucking bullshit. Earlier you texted me that you were okay, but now you have Drow fuckers on your ass?"

James grunted. "I wasn't lying. I didn't know they were *right* on my ass."

Shay groaned. "Don't die, asshole. The only person allowed to kill your ass is *me*. I'll get there and back you up. Somehow. Just... Just don't fucking die, okay? Hide until those AET assholes show up if you have to. Find some random tourists to feed them."

The bounty hunter let out a low chuckle. "This isn't exactly some Peruvian jungle. Not a lot of places to hide, and I'm not planning to die anyway. I was on a job, and I'm geared up. I have my amulet, so it's not like they can roll over me."

"Good, so you go full-Krypton on their asses. Maybe you'll get lucky and unlock a power or some shit."

James chuckled. "Don't think it works that way, but

here's hoping." He sighed. "Anyway, I just wanted to let you know how important you are to me, and how you've made me a better man. Promise me one thing."

"What?"

"That you'll take care of Alison."

"I don't need to make that promise because you're not gonna fucking die. You're gonna rip the spines out of those Drow bastards and make bongo drums out of their fucking skulls."

"Promise me," James thundered.

"I promise," Shay whispered back.

Both fell into silence, only their heavy breaths audible on either end of the line for several long moments.

Shay sighed. "James, if you die there, I'll never forgive you. I'm gonna hire a necromancer to bring you back just so I can kick your ass." She hung up.

The bounty hunter nodded. If that was the last thing Shay ever said to him in this life, it'd be fitting.

Should I even call Alison? Is it fair for her to feel afraid after what she went through with her mom?

He took a deep breath and dialed Alison. There was no way he could die without saying goodbye to his daughter.

"Hey, Dad," the teen answered. "I wasn't expecting you to call again so soon, but I guess you didn't pay attention to my warning, did you? You're in trouble. Bad trouble, I'm guessing."

"Huh? How did you know?"

"I just did. I can feel it somehow."

James shook his head. Somehow his women always seemed to know what was going on with him better than he did.

Maybe that's why I feel so much more alive now that you two are in my life.

"I thought about lying to you because you're far away and can't see me," he began, "but you deserve the truth. Three Drow are after me, and from what I've heard I don't think this little meet-up ends with them thanking me for looking after you."

Massive static filled the line for a few seconds. "I want to believe that you'll be okay, but I've been learning about them. Mom left them for a reason, and I also know my Drow side is darker and hungrier than my human side. I'm not saying they're all evil, but Dad, they *are* dangerous."

"Then you know I probably can't invite them to Jessie Rae's to talk this all out over some brisket. I don't want to fight them, Alison, but I'm not gonna be anyone's punching bag, even if you're related to them. I hope you can understand that."

"Family's about a lot more than blood. Walt and you both proved that to me in different ways." Alison laughed. "And family first, Dad. The others can suck it. Brownstone for the win, always. I hope you kick their asses all the way back to Oriceran."

James laughed.

"Remember, Dad, if you need it, you control the wish. You use it to survive."

"That's for you, not me. Not gonna die anyway, but on the off chance that it looks like I might, I'll consider it."

"If you die, I'm going to wish you back to life and then kick your butt for being stupid."

James laughed even harder than last time. "Okay there, Mini-Shay."

Alison let out a quiet sigh. "I love you, Dad."

"I love you, too, and I hope to see you soon." He ended the call and held the phone to his chest for a moment.

"I don't care how much it *costs*, Peyton," Shay shouted into her phone. "Just find someone who can do it. We live in a world crawling with magical assholes. I'm sure you can find one around here if you try hard enough. Don't call me back until you've found someone." She ended the call and took several deep breaths.

Her phone chimed with a text, and she glared at it, prepared to send Peyton a nasty text back. But it wasn't from him, it was from Alison.

I will wipe out every Drow in existence if they kill my dad. I will go to Oriceran and burn their houses to the ground with my magic.

Shay stared at the text. This wasn't just a kid talking. She swallowed and texted back. She needed to try and pull the girl back.

James couldn't have a better daughter than you. Don't worry. He's got a lot of backup coming. Your dad is gonna be okay.

Just hope we can get there in time.

"I might be coming to join you soon, Father Thomas. Unless they boot me down south."

Yea, though I walk through the valley of the shadow of death,

I will fear no evil: for thou art with me; thy rod and thy staff they comfort me.

James parked the F-350 behind a massive dune, stepped out, sighed, and threw on a backpack. Thankfully, the Professor's lead box containing the Clown of Doom was small enough to fit inside. He couldn't risk some random asshole thinking his truck was abandoned and grabbing it with a dangerous artifact inside. It'd suck to die and then be responsible for some city blowing up right after. God would probably frown on that for sure.

Unlike in Vegas with the Red-Eyes Killer, he had two major advantages going into the Drow confrontation. He'd expected a lot more trouble on the job, so he'd brought a standard layout, including his tactical harness, guns, multiple magazines, throwing knives, and grenades. Though he hadn't bothered to bring much in the way of electronic gadgets, he didn't expect that to be much of a disadvantage in a fight against the magical Drow.

"Wish I would have brought an RPG or two," James muttered. He finished checking his magazines and confirmed that he had his healing and energy potions in a pouch. As long as he could still move, he could survive.

Or they could just blow my fucking arms off, and then I'm screwed.

James stepped away from the truck, his boots leaving deep imprints as he marched toward the dry lakebed. He took a deep breath and reached under his shirt to yank the metal separator off the back of the amulet.

The amulet touched his skin, and pain spiked from his chest as the amulet sank into his flesh. Agony spread from his chest to every part of his body, and fire burnt every nerve. He took deep breaths through his clenched teeth as he waited for the pain to fade.

The agony receded, replaced by the dark whispers in the back of his mind. For the first time, James thought he could almost understand them.

Curiosity. That's what the amulet was feeling. Curiosity about an unfamiliar location.

"You like that shit?" James whispered. "Help keep my ass alive, and you'll have a chance to see a lot of new places. Three of them. Two of us. Let's do this shit."

He marched out onto the dry lakebed.

22

Zavan narrowed his eyes as he surveyed the dried-out lakebed from the front seat of the Porsche. Barren. Lifeless. It reminded him of the destroyed and withered lands of Oriceran still marked by the Great War, some scorched and lifeless even thousands of years later.

"Impressive," he murmured. "They lack in many areas, but they do have a talent for destruction. One has to respect that."

Reyal looked his way. "What?"

"The humans have destroyed an entire lake. That would have taken powerful magic to accomplish. Foolish in a way that only an Atlantean or human might do something, but then again the humans remind me of them in so many ways."

In the back seat, Kaella continued to stare at a pulsing black orb hovering above her hand. "Now that we've stopped moving, the suppression spell won't help so much.

If we're being watched, they'll soon find where we are because of the magical compass."

Zavan shook his head. "I'm not worried. The fools at the consulate have been weakened by spending too much time around humans. Even if they detect our magic and attempt to intervene, it'll be too late. We're close to him now. We'll defeat him and force the location of the princess out of him. By the time anyone comes looking, we'll have already found the princess."

Reyal stared off into the distance. "There's nothing here. Why would he come here?"

Zavan shrugged. "I suspect he's selected the battleground on which he wishes to die. There's little reason for him to travel to such a forsaken place otherwise."

"You think he knows we're following him?"

"I suspect as much. Perhaps his outwitting of the Widowmaker wasn't due to chance, as we thought. He must have access to powerful magical allies."

Reyal squinted. "There's so much sun here, and no buildings to hide in. A plan to distract and weaken us."

"By Brownstone?"

"Yes."

Zavan dismissed that outright. "His plans are worthless unless they keep us away from him. We're close now, so he's failed, and he will suffer for his failure."

Reyal glared at the sun as if she could frighten the star into setting. "Why couldn't we have done this somewhere far from this wretched sun-soaked land?"

Zavan snorted. "If Brownstone came here thinking a minor inconvenience would allow him victory, he's far more foolish than we realized. It doesn't matter. We have the cloaks, and we are three. He is but one. Being powerful for a human still means he's merely human."

Kaella used her free hand to grab three dark cloaks from behind the front passenger seat and passed them to her fellow Drow. They slipped them on, which required some twisting in the tight seating of the sports car.

"I hope Brownstone resists," Kaella murmured. "It won't be as much fun if he doesn't."

Zavan frowned. "Remember our orders. We need to find the princess. That should be foremost in our minds."

"We've wasted so much time waiting. We should have attacked him days ago."

"Waiting has left Brownstone far from his seat of power and allies. This way if battle is necessary we won't have outsiders interfering, and if he doesn't resist questioning there won't be others around to overhear."

Kaella snorted. "Questioning him is unnecessary. We can trace her essence from his corpse."

"Maybe. Such a spell isn't certain, though, and his magical allies have already proven to have enough power to block our other tracking spells." Zavan shook his head. "We won't make the same mistake Widowmaker did. Our pleasures will come after our duty and mission. The princess is key to the future of the Drow. Take pleasure from completing the will of our Queen. Everything else is secondary."

The Drow stepped out of the vehicle, their long dark hooded cloaks covering their features and protecting them from obnoxious rays of the sun.

Kaella grinned at the pulsing black orb, the magical compass guiding them straight to James Brownstone. "He's so close now. If he knew we were following him, he should have kept running and prayed to whatever gods he worships that we would never find him."

"Bravery," Zavan suggested. "Respectable, but in this case, ultimately futile."

"We're thirty minutes out from the LZ," the helicopter pilot announced.

Sergeant Mack wasn't sure if the LAPD borrowing National Guard choppers to go after Oricerans was remotely legal, but he figured he'd leave that discussion to people far above his pay grade.

The thump and judder of the helicopter as it cut through the sky made conversation difficult. The AET officers were all strapped into their seats, their armor ready and their helmets in their lap. Some carried pensive expressions, while others were excited.

Sergeant Mack sat next to Lieutenant Hall. He lacked full AET armor, but he did have a bulletproof vest—not that he thought it'd do him much good against magic.

He leaned toward the AET team leader. "Thanks for letting me come along, Lieutenant."

"I still don't think you get how dangerous this shit is going to be, Mack."

"I've been on plenty of scenes when AET took a guy down."

"Yeah, but these Drow make someone like King Pyro look like nothing. Even with deflectors, many of my guys ended up in the hospital the last time we tangled with one.

This time it's a triple threat." She narrowed her eyes at him. "I only said yes because I didn't need a bunch of drama right as we were taking off, but that changes *nothing*. You stay the hell behind us. You have a chance for a lucky shot, then be my fucking guest, but you try to be a hero out there against any of those three monsters? They'll kill you like nothing. You got me?"

"Yeah, I got you. But last time you fought a Drow you didn't have Brownstone helping you."

"Even the Scourge of Harriken is just a man in the end, Mack."

"And those Drow are just fancy elves. Magic may make you powerful, but it doesn't make you immortal."

Lieutenant Hall nodded. "Let's damn well hope so, for everyone's sake."

James stood in the center of the dried lakebed, waiting as the dark cloaked figures closed on him. He doubted he'd survive the next hour.

Fuck, should have brought a water bottle with me. I'm thirsty.

The amulet whispered in his mind, but he was back to not being able to understand it.

I wonder if you actually say anything useful.

He pulled out his phone. No cell signal. The AET had depended on his phone to track him. He hoped they could at least spot his truck and follow his trail from there.

What the fuck does it matter? They aren't here now, and the Drow are. Thanks, Lieutenant Hall. At least you tried, but somehow I knew this shit would come down to me and these sonsabitches.

There was still the chance he was wrong and the Drow didn't want to fight him, or have anything to do with Alison. Maybe they were just Oriceran fans of his. A man could always hope.

James let his hands drop to his sides and waited for the Drow to move nearer. They closed to ten yards, and he frowned.

He'd been expecting dark skin, white hair, and red eyes, but instead, he saw three normal-looking humans. Almost *too* normal. Bland humans in suits with no distinguishing characteristics other than the dark cloaks they were wearing.

"Shapeshifting?" James called.

The tallest, a man, shook his head. "A simple illusion spell. It lacks the depth of modification used by Widowmaker."

"Widowmaker? Who the fuck is that?"

The man chuckled. "Ah, the Drow assassin you had your allies eliminate."

James grimaced. "A nickname. Of *course* she had a fucking nickname, and who are you supposed to be, the Terrible Trio?"

One of the women glared at him. "Watch your tongue, human, or I'll remove it."

The man silenced her with a raised arm. "His attitude is amusing. Let's respect his bravery, Kaella."

"As you say, Zavan."

James looked between the two of them. "Actual names. Nice." He nodded toward the other woman. "And her?"

"I am Reyal," she declared.

"Guess you know who I am, already, huh?"

Zavan nodded. "James Brownstone, a man they some-times call the Granite Ghost and the Scourge of Harriken. You've earned many impressive victories and titles, Brownstone."

"Not my fault. People keep fucking with me. I just try to mind my own business." He shrugged. "Speaking of which, why are you all so interested in me?"

Zavan smiled. "We bear you no ill will, Brownstone. We simply seek to recover that which belongs to our people, and to do that we must find the Princess of the Shadow Forged. We know she's on Earth. We know she was in Los Angeles, and we know you were in contact with her."

James grunted. The next part was going to be more than a little awkward.

"First of all," he began, "and let me make this shit clear—I didn't kill her, but she's dead. Those Harriken guys, the ones I'm the scourge of, they tortured her. But you don't have to worry, I've destroyed almost all the Harriken. They're done as a group. I got her revenge."

Zavan, Reyal, and Kaella exchanged glances.

The Drow man chuckled and shook his head, still in his bland human disguise. "No, not the last princess. When her mother died, the title passed to the daughter. Where is the girl?"

James' hands tightened into fists and his heart beat faster. The amulet whispered in his mind. This time he could somewhat understand it. It wanted to fight. It wanted to test itself against the new foes.

You're just a masochist, huh? Do you even give a shit that we might not be able to win?

The amulet whispered something—a denial, perhaps.

"Why do you even want her?" James countered.

Pretending he didn't even know about Alison seemed pointless. The Drow had traveled all the way from Oriceran and tracked him down. Magic or simple investigation, they obviously already knew he was in contact with her.

Zavan shrugged. "It's as I said—she's the new Princess of the Shadow Forged. Her destiny and duty lie with her people." He pointed to his heart. "With us. Among other things, we suspect that her magical education has been neglected. Can you claim that you can offer that?"

"Me? Fuck no, but I know people who can, and she's with them now."

"I see. That would explain why we've had such trouble tracking her down."

James' gaze flicked between the three. No one's hands were tensed and ready to go for a weapon or throw off a magical bolt. That could be a good thing in that they weren't ready to fight, or a bad thing in that they held him in such contempt they didn't think they needed to be ready to do so.

How do I know they are even bad? They might just be assholes. It's all rumors. Maybe they are just misunderstood.

The amulet hissed in his mind, urging him toward battle.

"Maybe we could talk about you meeting her," James suggested. "With some rules and limits, and if she agrees to it."

"Agrees to it? Her queen demands it. There is no 'agreeing to it.'"

James snorted. "See, that just shows that you don't know her. I'm not gonna force a traumatized girl to be jerked around by a bunch of adults for political shit."

"Political shit?" Kaella sneered. "Brownstone just wants the legacy. Greedy, like all of his kind."

"That's bullshit. That's not even mine. That's hers."

The Drow woman smiled. "So he *does* know of the legacy."

Shit. That probably didn't help things.

Zavan took a single step forward, his smile disappearing. "We have our orders. The princess' opinion is irrelevant. She will return to Oriceran and rejoin the Drow. She will not be polluted by further manipulations by humans and other weak races."

James grunted. "Fuck, Zavan. I thought we had a good discussion going, and now you have to go and be a little magical Nazi."

He snorted. "I've read about your Nazis. They were weak humans in uniforms. We are Drow. We are all strong."

Reyal's fingers twitched.

Yeah, almost go time.

The amulet all but shouted in James' mind.

Kaella spat on the ground. "This is a waste. You're nothing, Brownstone—a pathetic and weak human who has lucked into victories against pathetic and weak opponents. You know of the legacy, and it is your greed that motivates you, not care for the princess. You think you can use that wish, human?"

James pointed at Kaella. "I don't want or need her fucking wish. I didn't even ask to be the caretaker of it. Her mom made me. I've told the girl about it, but she hasn't made up her mind about what she wants to use it for."

Kaella's eyes bulged. "It's not hers to use on frivolous matters. It is for our people, to be used at the discretion of the queen."

The three Drow spread out, their legs bent and their hands up.

"This is your last chance, Brownstone," Zavan announced. "Tell us where the princess is. If you don't, you won't even be given the dignity of a quick death. We will assure your death is slow and painful."

James sighed and shook his head. "You're a real fucked-up piece of shit. If this is what the Drow are like, I don't want Alison anywhere near them."

"Alison? That's her name. Interesting. You won't win, Brownstone. You think because Widowmaker was beaten, you'll win? She was an assassin. She struck best when the target was unaware. We're not assassins. We are warriors."

Kaella lifted her hands, and a cloud of black energy enveloped them. "It's time we beat the stupid human." A nimbus of dark energy surrounded her body. "After we torture you and get the information we need, I will enjoy feeding on your soul."

James gestured for her to attack. "Let's see what you got."

The Drow charged with a sick grin on her face. James met her with a full-force punch in the chest. Kaella flew back several yards and hit the ground, rolling to a stop a few feet away. She growled and pushed herself off the ground.

James gave her a polite nod. "If I'd hit a human that hard, he'd probably be dead now. You're tough." He cracked his knuckles. "But I'm beginning to wonder if I'm tougher."

The amulet's joy spilled into his mind.

Yeah, you're gonna get your ass-kicking time, you sick piece of shit.

The Drow all whipped their cloaks off and tossed them to the ground, squinting under the sun's ray. They shimmered for a moment, and the three bland humans in suits vanished, replaced by three dark-skinned, white-haired, red-eyed Drow with long pointed ears. They all wore tight-fitting armor composed of tightly overlapping dark scales with an almost carapace-like appearance. Dark energy fields surrounded all three, and blades of pure shadow extended from their arms.

"Have you ever flayed a man, Brownstone?" Zavan asked, his wide smile revealing gleaming white teeth. "Slowly, surely, you can peel away the man's skin and his will. I wonder how long it'll take with you. Hours? Days? Weeks? Do you have the will to last months, even?"

"I think we should start with his manhood," Kaella suggested.

Reyal shook her head. "Blind him first. The anticipation of pain as he hears us near him will make it hurt worse."

James grimaced. "You are some sick fucks, but are you going to boast, or you just going to toast out here in the sun?"

23

Reyal charged this time, ducking James' fist and slashing with a shadow blade extending from her arm. Despite the ephemeral appearance, it sliced open his shirt and chest like any other solid blade and burned, not from heat, but from intense cold.

The amulet's joy flooded his mind, unnerving him.

Fucking masochist. It's my damned body getting shredded.

James hissed and jumped back, whipping out his .45. He pulled the trigger several times. Reyal jerked back and stumbled, but no actual holes appeared in her armor or body.

The bounty hunter kept firing, backpedaling until his gun clicked empty. He ejected the magazine and loaded a new one. The Drow had gotten the better of him in that exchange.

Zavan and Kaella continued to watch and not intervene, faint smiles on their faces.

You fuckers think I'm so weak that you don't need to gang up on me?

James unloaded his new magazine into Reyal. Each strike seemed to land, but when his gun finally clicked empty a second time, only a few spots of blood marred the ground. A single hole in her armor and flesh sealed itself within seconds.

James ejected the magazine and reloaded again. "That's fucking annoying."

Reyal grinned and circled him. "Do you not yet understand, Brownstone? Mere strength is insufficient. You're powerful for a human, but nothing against a Drow."

James snorted. "Do you have any idea how many times I've heard a variation of that fucking speech?"

"I don't care. You've not faced us before."

Reyal rushed forward and slashed again.

The bounty hunter brought up his arm to block on instinct.

Shit, this isn't some Harriken katana. Guess I'll find out if a healing potion can grow my arm back.

The blade sliced into his sleeve but bounced off his skin like he'd expect from any metal sword.

Reyal frowned and stabbed for her next attack. It stung, but didn't leave more than a scratch. James put two rounds into her and backhanded her when she was recovering from the shots. The Drow flew through the air with a groan.

Overjoyed. That's what the amulet felt. That was what it was whispering about. He was sure of it.

James holstered his pistol and chuckled, his stomach unknotting itself as his confidence returned. "Fuck, and I was even starting to let myself get worried." He winced. The original slice still ached, but the other blows had barely scratched him. "Guess you should have cut my head off when you had the chance, assholes."

Reyal hopped off the ground, her nimbus darkening around her. She wiped the blood off her face as her cuts sealed themselves.

Zavan thrust out his arm and an inky bolt of darkness flew toward James. The bounty hunter didn't even bother to dodge, convinced his amulet could take the hit.

The bolt tore through his left shoulder and knocked him back. He grunted as he hit the ground, pain shooting through his arm and shoulder. He hissed and forced himself back to his feet.

Would you make up your fucking mind?

The amulet's whispers grew loud and insistent.

The Drow smiled. "Arrogance has felled much greater warriors than you, James Brownstone. You should also understand that we're restraining ourselves."

"What, am I supposed to give you a fucking medal or something?"

"We still have need of something from you. Otherwise, this farce would have already ended with your body in shreds." Zavan shook his head. "Cease your arrogant resistance. I no longer find it amusing."

With a grimace, James inspected his shoulder wound. The hole went all the way through and burned, but no blood dripped from it. A thin layer of ice coated the damage.

"Fuck you," offered James. "You've got no business bitching about me being arrogant, you sonofabitch."

Something thumped in the distance, but James kept his attention on the Drow. He took several steps back and grabbed a grenade. He tossed it toward Zavan but not directly at the ground before yanking out a K-Bar and sprinting forward.

The grenade exploded, knocking all three Drow to the ground. James changed direction, now heading straight toward Zavan. He leapt, his grip tightened around the knife, as he slammed the knife into the Drow's chest.

Zavan howled and shoved his hands forward, dark energy emerging from the palms. James flew backward, the front of his chest shredded. He landed on the ground with a thud and hopped to his feet, taking deep breaths.

His arm and chest ached, and blood poured from several wounds in his chest.

"Come on," James yelled. "All that talk about how badass you are, and I'm still moving? I've fought tougher street thugs than you assholes."

The amulet continued to whisper. By now James could discern the happy texture of the mental communication with ease. At least someone was enjoying the fight.

Zavan stood, swaying on unsteady feet, pieces of shrapnel embedded in his body and face. The dark field around him was less dense than the two women's. Their wounds were already closing. He coughed up blood and laughed.

James matched his laugh. "What's wrong, badass? I thought you could just heal, but it looks like I've fucked you up."

"I'll grant you some small modicum of respect. A lesser being would have died from that attack. You're of far studier stock than we anticipated. I wouldn't go so far as to call you a worthy foe, but at least you're mildly diverting."

The bounty hunter kept his grin on his face, but his left arm was useless. With the Drow so close, he couldn't go for his healing potion. He also needed a better strategy. The grenade and stabbing had wounded Zavan, but the asshole was still up and spewing bullshit. The women were barely touched.

I can't win like this. Maybe if I can go for the throat?

Zavan sneered. "We can keep you alive and in agony for far longer than you could imagine."

"That's why I'm the nicer guy. I'm just gonna fucking kill you quick-like."

The Drow all raised a hand behind them and thrust them forward in unison. Three dark bolts shot toward James and slammed into him. He grunted, but unlike the first shadow bolt attack, the energy projectiles didn't pierce his body. They dissipated like smoke on the wind. Only the jolt of the impact near his original chest wounds produced pain.

The trio frowned and launched another volley. James grunted and stepped back. He fired a couple of rounds into Reyal and Kaella to force them back and then emptied the rest of his clip into Zavan. The Drow jerked several times and collapsed to his knees coughing up blood.

Just need to overwhelm their defenses. Damn. Wish I had a magical sword about now. I could have already won. Fucking Drow.

James sprinted to the side and fired off a few more rounds before tossing another grenade. This time the dark fields around the Drow shifted to opaque domes. The grenade exploded, and when the flame and smoke cleared, the three enemies remained unaffected.

Zavan sucked in deep, labored breaths. "The problem with any trick is that it only works once." Some of the shrapnel fell out, and the wounds began to close.

"I could say the same thing, asshole." He winced at the throbbing in his chest and shoulder. "How about this?" The bounty hunter holstered his pistol and tried a throwing knife. The knife bounced off his dark field and fell to the ground.

Zavan had the gall to roll his fucking eyes at James.

I'm so gonna smash your smug Drow face in, you asshole.

James reached for his K-Bar and realized he no longer had it. It lay on the ground several feet away. He hadn't even realized he'd lost it during Zavan's shadow shotgun attack.

Reyal and Kaella charged either side of him, slashing with shadow blades. Gritting his teeth, James forced his left arm to parallel his right as he blocked the attacks. The slashes stung but didn't bite deeply into his skin. The two Drow women followed up with two quick slashes and a stab each. He booted Reyal to the side and threw his elbow into Kaella's face, sending her crashing to the sand.

Both scrambled back to their feet, murder in their red eyes.

What's with me and fighting red-eyed assholes lately?

Fuck. Zavan's the only one I've even slowed down, and he's already healing. Maybe I should run and take the potion. If I can use my left arm, at least I'll have a chance.

Kaella's shadow blade disappeared. She raised one hand above her. Blue-Green flames appeared around it. Reyal matched the gesture, as did Zavan. A moment later, a blast of blue-green energy shot from each of them in a coordinated attack on James' left leg.

Burning agony consumed his leg, and James fell to one knee. The joint Drow attack had left a large hole in his pants, but it hadn't pierced his leg like the shadow bolts. Instead, a good quarter of an inch of tissue was missing, like they'd taken gritty magical sandpaper to his upper leg.

James took several deep breaths and forced himself back to his feet. "You fuckers need to finish me off if you want to win. Otherwise, I'm just gonna keep getting back up and ruining your day."

They didn't move. Instead, another joint attack blasted into his other leg. The energy burned another hole, but only singed the top of his leg.

The amulet's whispers had vanished, replaced by blasts of emotion, or at least that's how James perceived it. Happiness. Satisfaction.

James grunted, having noticed an important pattern.

Guess you fuckers only get one shot before Mr. Masochist figures it out.

He stumbled toward his K-Bar on the ground. Tenebrous blasts shot from behind the Drow, and the trio flew toward him with their legs out. They crashed into him with powerful kicks, sending him to the ground but not accomplishing much other than annoying him and making his existing wounds ache.

They followed with intricate movements of their arms and hands. Dozens of small black orbs blasted from the dark nimbuses surrounding the Drow and pelted James, stinging and burning him. When they struck an uninjured area he barely noticed, but more than a few slammed into his wounded leg, arm, and chest.

Fuck.

James groaned, the pain building. The Drow pressed the attack, a hungry gleam in their eyes.

"I'm impressed, Brownstone," Zavan managed after coughing up more blood. "You should be dead many times over, yet you still are moving. No human is this tough. I sense something odd about you, but I can't begin to explain it. It's like nothing I've ever encountered."

"Glad I could fucking entertain you," James managed through gritted teeth.

The bounty hunter fell to one knee. The Drow changed their movements, and the orbs separated into dozens of smaller pellets before hitting James.

He hissed in pain, falling forward. He'd been able to ignore and gut-check past his pain before, but the near constant bombardment of the shadow comets left his entire body screaming, every nerve cell on fire.

The amulet had finally gone silent both in whisper and emotion.

Even you have your limits, Mr. Masochist?

The Drow attack finally ended. Kaella marched up to James and glared down at him. She reared back, and impenetrable darkness surrounded her foot. Another powerful kick snapped his head back and sent him flying.

James rolled several times following his hard impact, the motion jarring his other wounds.

He used his good arm to push himself up. He managed a weak snort. "What's wrong, Zavan? Letting the women do all the work?"

Shit. Glad Shay wasn't here. I'd never fucking hear the end of it.

Zavan's steps remained unsteady and not all his wounds were healed, but he looked far less pained than earlier. James was losing the war of attrition.

"You've lost, Brownstone." Zavan let out a dark chuckle. "But this defensive magic you have is exquisite. It'll serve our purposes well, and it'll make torturing you all that more interesting."

"Glad I could bring a smile to your face."

Kaella thrust her palm forward. A dense black orb shot toward James. It exploded in a ball of blue-green fire and knocked him back. Blood dripped from several new wounds.

The amulet broke its silence with an excited whisper.

Every part of the bounty hunter's body throbbed. It was hard to concentrate, and his vision wavered.

Zavan stepped in front of Kaella and put his arm out. "Don't kill him. We still need to question him. Besides, it'll be more entertaining to kill him slowly."

Maria rested the railgun over her armored shoulder. She slid back the charging bolt and waited for the telltale hum.

"Work, you damned piece of junk. I've got some Drow to waste."

You should watch your backs better, assholes.

She squeezed the trigger, and the loaded round roared out of the weapon. Zavan didn't even have time to look before a hypervelocity shot slammed into him. He flew through the air with a new hole in his chest.

Maria ducked when Reyal and Kaella blasted shadow bolts at her. The other AET officers charged from opposite sides, opening fire with stun and assault rifles. Bullets rained on the three Drow.

The lieutenant would have loved to have the help of a few rocket drones, but hitching a ride with the National Guard meant leaving a lot of equipment back home. It was obvious Brownstone would have been a corpse if they'd tried to drive to the Salton Sea.

James crawled away. Even from a distance, Maria could tell he was torn up.

Fuck. Sorry, Brownstone, we got here ASAP.

He reached into a pouch on his singed tactical belt and pulled out a tiny glass bottle.

A healing potion? That's some expensive shit, Brownstone.

James gulped down the contents of the bottle.

"Need to distract them so he can heal," Maria radioed.

The other AET officers continued to rain fire on the Drow, but they didn't seem to be doing much damage. Maria threw a sonic grenade at Zavan, but it bounced off the shield dome he'd erected.

Thirty seconds later, James' clothes looked like he'd been run through a shredder, but his wounds were gone. He jumped to his feet and scooped his knife off the ground.

Yeah, Brownstone. I'm not going to let you ever forget how I saved your ass. Now help end this shit.

Maria readied another railgun round and initiated the charging cycle on the weapon. The unreliable piece of junk might not be her first choice in a fight, but it packed a punch.

Reyal leapt into the air, four wings of shadow springing from her back. Bullets pelted her, and she hissed. A wave of exploding black orbs shot from her hands, forcing several of the AET back.

James opened fire on the flying Drow, forcing her attention to him.

"Brownstone, why won't you die already?" she shrieked.

Maria snickered. *I've asked myself that so many times.*

The Drow's wings vanished, and she dropped to the ground, landing on one knee with a smirk, a wave of black energy blasting around her. The energy knocked back several nearby AET officers, their deflectors darkening.

Shit, not again!

Maria relaxed when the men crawled to their feet. A few had to be helped, but no one was dead, and none of the deflectors were shattered.

We can win this shit, even with three of these Drow bastards. We'll show them the power of humans.

Reyal crossed her arms in front of her and thrust out. A massive blue-green orb of flame shot toward James, crackling and roaring.

Maria grimaced as the fireball exploded around the bounty hunter and sent his body tumbling, his clothes smoldering. His backpack slipped off, its straps mere burning threads now, and a small box flew out, smashed on the ground and cracked open. Something spilled out of it.

James pushed off the ground, not acting like a man who'd been in the heart of an explosion. His expression was more annoyed than pained.

You're one tough sonofabitch, Brownstone.

The lieutenant activated her goggles' magnification mode and focused on the contents of the box. Had the bounty hunter brought along some secret and powerful magical artifact? They could use any advantage.

Wait. Is that a damned clown figurine? What the fuck, Brownstone? You were out antiquing when Drow were hunting you?

Kaella screamed in frustration. She charged up the

sloping lakebed toward several AET officers. Their stun bolts and bullets did little to slow her.

The railgun hummed.

"Now we're talking," Maria murmured. She aimed at the charging Drow and blasted her. Kaella spun several times in the air before hitting the ground. She pushed herself up, shadowy tendrils beginning to knit the hole in her leg closed.

Zavan pushed himself off the ground, his previous wounds all but gone, though his movements were slower than before. He flung out his arm. A half-dozen black orbs shot toward Maria, exploding around her and knocking her to the ground.

She blinked, trying to clear the stars out of her eyes. She hissed at the pain and glanced down at her deflector. It was cloudy but still functional. Her armor was scorched and pitted, and one of her lenses was cracked. The railgun was bent, with part of the metal melted.

More expensive shit they are going to bitch at me about. Maybe the next one we buy will work better.

"All units, I'm going to provide you some cover," Maria transmitted through her headset. "When I give the signal, switch to your anti-magic bullet magazines." *And even more expensive shit.* "And trust me, you'll know the signal when you see it."

Maria grabbed a small pink gem from her tactical belt —a little gift from Dannec.

Time for a Light Elf surprise, assholes.

She arced the gem toward the Drow. A few yards out it exploded in a shower of scintillating particles. The Drow hissed and rushed backward, their arms in front of their faces, their shadowy auras weakening.

"Now," Maria transmitted.

Every man and woman on the team ejected their magazines and loaded the new ones in three fluid motions. The power of proper training.

"Light their asses up!"

Bullets ripped from the rifles and slammed into the Drow. They jerked and hissed as the enchanted rounds tore through their bodies, their shadow magic struggling to keep up.

James jerked his head around until he spotted the Clown of Doom half-buried in the ground. He jogged toward the figurine. It wouldn't do any good to survive the Drow attack if the entire area all went up in a magical mushroom crowd.

On the plus side, at least they weren't in a city.

He rotated his left arm a few times. It didn't matter how many times he used a healing potion. He was always surprised at how effective they were.

Thanks, Zoe. You saved my life yet again.

Rifles cracked as the AET rained death on the three Drow. Bullet wounds covered their bodies, but they remained stubbornly standing. Zavan's shadow nimbus spread out to form a translucent dome around them. He murmured something to the women, and they looked James' way, sneering.

The AET officers fired for about ten more seconds

before realizing their bullets couldn't pierce the shield. The two Drow women didn't launch any attacks from the inside.

Reyal and Kaella joined hands and glared at James.

What the fuck are they doing? Why did they stop attacking? Maybe they can't. Total defense, no offense? Siege time?

Lieutenant Hall aimed a pistol at them. "This is Lieutenant Maria Hall of the LAPD AET. Drop all spells immediately and put your hands above your head."

Zavan ignored the lieutenant and laughed, wild-eyed, his shield still in place. "You said it before, Brownstone, but I didn't even realize it until now. It's why I felt some strange pushback from you. I let my own arrogance blind me to the mission."

"What the fuck are you talking about, Zavan?" James pointed at Lieutenant Hall. "Don't you get it, asshole? You've lost. That's why you're pulling this shadow turtle bullshit. The minute you drop that shield, AET finishes turning you into Swiss cheese."

"It doesn't matter. The legacy's what is important. That's *all* the queen cares about. The wish is the key to our future. The next few decades are critical."

"Well, duh. What's your fucking point, asshole? You can't get the wish if you're dead. You surrender right now, and maybe you'll weasel out with some diplomatic immunity bullshit."

The idea annoyed James, but he was fine with anything that would stop the immediate fight. They'd only been lucky no cops had been killed.

Zavan coughed up blood. More oozed from several wounds all over his body. "But the princess doesn't have the legacy anymore, and the Drow don't need half-human trash as a Princess of the Shadow Forged polluting our people." He locked eyes with James. "We will just yank the legacy from you and leave this wretched place."

The AET opened fire again, but it wasn't a steady stream. A shot here and a shot there, as if they were probing the Drow's defenses, probably via radio order through their helmet comms.

Still holding each other's hand, the two Drow women stretched out their free arms.

"You were a fool to oppose the Drow, Brownstone," Zavan shouted. "If you're fortunate, this won't shred your soul."

Two bolts of energy, one blue, one green, shot from Reyal and Kaella's respective hands. They twisted around each other, their shuddering and twitching lines of energy joining together to form a larger blast, one headed straight toward James.

"Oh, shit!"

A few seconds passed before James registered that he wasn't dead. He should have been dead. Two Drow had conjured a spell to drain Alison's wish from him, after all—not to mention the promised shredding of his soul.

Instead, he was standing there staring at the Drow, who looked as confused as James felt. It was then that he realized something was pulsing brightly on the ground. The glow was accompanied by a building whine.

The Clown of Doom. Somehow the artifact had absorbed the magical release.

Not only was it pulsing and whining, but a moment of observation confirmed the pulse rate and volume were increasing. James' gaze jerked from the figurine to the Drow.

"Fuck." James jumped to the ground and grabbed the figurine. He hissed as his skin sizzled from the intense heat of the artifact. With quality World Series-form, he pitched the pulsing Clown of Doom straight at the Drow and their protective dome, clinging to some vague hope that the entire area wouldn't go up in a magical explosion.

Lines of energy flowed from Kaella and Reyal into the dome, strengthening it.

Hell, at least this way I know Alison will be safe. No Drow are ever gonna come looking for her after learning these three got blown up by a magical nuke.

The Clown of Doom collided with the shield and shattered, producing a blinding flash. The erupting shockwave slammed into James. His eyes were still adjusting and ears ringing when he crashed to the ground.

James groaned, his stomach churning and his head throbbing. He sat up and blinked.

"Wait, I'm not fucking dead." He looked back and forth. Several AET officers, including Lieutenant Hall, were picking themselves up off the ground. The lieutenant took off her cracked and seared helmet and tossed it to the ground. The barrel of her pistol was melted, and the other cop's guns hadn't fared much better.

James fished out his gun. Strange. The barrel and grip were warped and melted, but the holster didn't show any signs of new burns.

Not an explosion, then. More like some reality-warping shit?

The bounty hunter shook his head. He didn't want to even *begin* to think about something like that, especially with the ringing in his ears.

The three Drow were defeated. Kaella and Reyal lay on the ground, or at least their burnt husks did. Zavan's still flesh-covered body lay face down on the ground.

Throwing the Professor's ultimate artifact at the trio hadn't been on the top of James' smartest plans ever, but it'd done the trick. All the good guys were alive, and the bad guys were dead.

The amulet whispered quietly in James' mind. Satisfied, maybe.

Or smug.

James could only assume that he hadn't been burned to a crisp because of the amulet.

"Is everyone all right?" Lieutenant Hall called.

The other AET officer moaned their affirmative answers. Not a single man or woman remained on the ground, except the three charred Drow.

Even though James wasn't extra-crispy like the Drow, weariness infused every muscle in his body; perhaps a side-effect of being so close to the explosion's epicenter. He could handle a little fatigue. Fuck, he was more than happy to take a nap like a preschooler in his truck after the shit he'd just been through.

I guess the only important shit is that, in the end, those Drow assholes got what was coming to them. Fuckers.

Zavan stirred and pushed himself to his knees, then his feet.

James groaned. "You've got to be fucking kidding me."

For a brief moment, he understood what other people felt like when they complained about him not dying.

The Drow turned to face James. The wounded elf trembled and swayed, having obvious difficulty standing. Blood ran freely now from his wounds. Pieces of his body winked in and out of existence, and he hissed in pain.

"Have you seen it, Brownstone?" Zavan croaked. "Did the princess show you how you can feed the magic with a soul, but feeding it with your own soul is even more powerful?"

"It's over, Zavan. Give it up."

He threw both arms out to the side. Bright lines of energy webbed across the air and a circular wall of light shot into the air, trapping everyone inside it.

"What the fuck are you doing?" James shouted.

"My duty, human. If the legacy is to be denied the Drow, then I shall ensure it is denied to *all*." Pieces of his body continued to disappear and reappear. "I don't know what you used, or why you had it." He screamed in pain. He laughed a second later. "You've thinned the walls between dimensions, but they already are starting to thicken. I can feel it. I'm sending us all away first."

James grunted. "You think you're gonna get Drow reinforcements on Oriceran?"

The bounty hunter tried to stand, only for his knees to give out.

"Oriceran? Oh, no. Not even the World in Between. It traps, but does not destroy enough. I'll use my soul and the thin walls to send us all to a much darker place." The wall of light turned scarlet, and a massive glowing portal appeared in the sky. James couldn't make out anything through the hole other than a thick gray mist that boiled with a mass of shadowy tentacles.

I'm sorry, Alison, I guess I'm gonna have to use your inheritance after all. If it was just me, that's one thing, but not all these other guys.

The AET officers all scrambled to look for a working weapon, but no one found one. Everyone had been too close to the artifact explosion.

"I've gotten partial to Earth," James muttered. He took a deep breath. "I wish that—"

A loud crack from behind accompanied Zavan's head exploding like an overly ripe watermelon under a sledgehammer, and his body slumped to the ground. The dimensional hole above him sealed itself in a matter of seconds, and the wall of light faded from existence.

James stared at the body, confused about what had happened. He wasn't sure how much time had passed when he heard someone call out from behind him.

"Brownstone? You are still alive, right? I'm not captaining PFW by myself."

James looked behind him. Sergeant Mack stood in the distance, a sniper rifle in his hands and an expression of awe on his face.

Mack laughed. "The bullet I just used cost more than my entire year's salary."

James offered him a wave and collapsed. "Fuck fighting in the sand and the sun."

The sun had given up, and the darkness that choked the area was broken only by the red and white lights of police cars and ambulances. Tight knots of AET officers in warped armor waited in ambulances for treatment or chatted with sheriff's deputies and highway patrol officers.

Shay grimaced. There were too many cops there for a dead hitman who'd died again recently, but she had to take the risk. James wasn't answering his phone.

Her heart thundered. Even though Peyton had located a wizard who could gate her directly to California for a ridiculous amount of money, she'd obviously arrived for the aftermath.

You were supposed to wait *for me, James. Dumbass.*

None of the cops present were paying any attention to her, which helped. Shay made her way toward the ambulances. If James had been hurt, that would be the best place to check.

"Stop whining like a baby, Weber," a female AET officer

with dark hair commented to another AET member with only the bottom of his armor on. Burns covered the top of his body. A paramedic was inspecting his wounds and applying spray.

"I don't even get it, Lieutenant," Weber replied. "You were closer, and you got hurt less."

"I know how to duck better than you, dumbass." She clapped him on the shoulder in the one spot that looked untouched. "Good job today, though."

"Thanks, Lieutenant."

The female AET officer turned and Shay winced, recognizing Lieutenant Maria Hall. The tomb raider rushed toward an ambulance.

Hall narrowed her eyes and jogged after Shay. "Hey, you—wait up!"

Shay's hand dropped inside her jacket and rested on the grip of her 9mm. She moved between two ambulances.

"I said fucking *stop!*" Hall shouted from behind Shay.

The tomb raider took several deep breaths and turned around.

The AET lieutenant stared at Shay, her mouth open. "What the fuck?"

I'm gonna have to kill her, but if I do, what the fuck will James say? There's no way he's gonna forgive me for killing a cop.

Lieutenant Hall took a few steps forward but didn't shout for reinforcements or charge Shay.

"Are you actually a fucking human, or are you another Drow?" the cop asked.

"Some people have called me a monster, but last time I checked I'm a human."

The cop tilted her head. "Yeah, you'd have to be. No way a Drow wouldn't have just gone to town to slaughter all our wounded asses. You're her, then. The real one." She snorted. "I fucking *knew* I was right about Brownstone having help."

Shay swallowed, her heart thumping.

I have to do it, James. If she blows my cover, it won't just be cops I'm having to deal with. Even with the cartel gone, it'll be dangerous, not just for me, but for Peyton.

Lieutenant Hall snorted. "You've got nothing to say?"

"What do you want me to say?"

"Brownstone's a lot of things, but he's not a hitman. Even *I* get now that he's only killed people who had it coming. So where do you fit in?"

Shay shrugged. "I'm not a hitman either. Not anymore. I can honestly say that woman is dead and buried."

The AET officer stared at Shay in silence for an uncomfortably long time before looking over her shoulder to confirm no one else was present and stepping closer to the tomb raider.

Lieutenant Hall shrugged. "I don't like to admit I'm wrong since it gives idiots like Weber ideas, but I was wrong about Brownstone. Take care of him. He's a good man."

Shay blinked and let her hand drift away from her gun. "Take care of him?"

"Yeah, I doubt some hot chick like you is hanging around a guy like Brownstone without him dipping his wick. A woman who is willing to take on a high-end killer to protect a man gives a major shit about him." The cop shrugged. "Look, I'll never admit I said he's a good man, so don't go saying that to anyone." She chuckled. "Not that a twice-dead hitman is going to go blabbing."

"It'd be a dumbass move." Shay grinned.

"I'm not going to bother asking you your name. I don't even know if something like that means much to a woman like you, but I do want to know one thing."

"What's that?"

"If you're not a hitman anymore, then what are you?"

"A tomb raider. And it's not like no one knows my name. You can call me Shay Carson."

Hall scrutinized her. "And are you thinking about becoming Shay Brownstone?"

Shay followed the cop's gaze. Relief flooded her. James stood by an ambulance with his phone pressed to his ear. Shay assumed it was Alison on the other end by his body language.

"Maybe, but I think I'll keep my name. Girl power, and all that shit. You probably understand."

"Sure." Lieutenant Hall chuckled. "Brownstone and I have come to an understanding, and I don't think I'm going mess that up by trying to take down his woman." Hall shrugged. "Besides, the woman who looked like you is dead, and the woman with your DNA is dead. There's no point in digging up the dead. Just don't do shit in my jurisdiction and we won't have a problem."

"Fair enough."

Hall gestured toward James. "I also wouldn't hang out here too long. It'll raise too many questions, and just because I'm willing to look the other way doesn't mean every cop is."

"Thanks." Shay gave the other woman a polite nod and made her way to James.

He brightened as he spotted her. Shay walked over to him and looked him up and down. He had on a borrowed cop's jacket, but his pants and shirt looked like someone had blasted him with a flamethrower and a shotgun several times.

"You look like shit," she observed.

James shrugged. "Three Drow tried to kill me, then a clown blew up."

Shay blinked. "A clown blew up?"

"Yeah, the Clown of Doom. Long story. Involves barbeque at one point. And dwarf mobsters."

She laughed. "Of course it does." She threw her arms around him and leaned in to whisper into his ear, "Next time, wait for me."

The deputies exchanged glances.

"Who is this?" one of them asked.

James smiled. "My girlfriend."

"Damn, Brownstone, your girl is a hottie."

The other deputy elbowed the first.

"Just sayin'."

Shay opened her mouth to object but closed it. Being friendly didn't mean she was blowing her cover. It wasn't like she needed to hang out with the cops going forward. For the moment, she'd let James have the pretty woman on his arm and not worry. It wasn't like James had mentioned her warehouses or her tomb-raiding alias.

Maybe in the future when her past was truly behind her, she'd be able to befriend cops. It'd take a long time for her to trust the people she'd hidden from for years, but this was a start.

James has lived in the open, so he can have normal friends. I'm still trapped in the shadows, but I'm crawling toward the sunlight with his help. Maybe that's what love does—makes us better people.

She gave him a kiss on his cheek.

"What was that for?"

Shay grinned. "Not dying. Now I don't have to spend money on a necromancer."

James turned to the deputies. "My girlfriend threatened that if I got killed, she was gonna hire a necromancer to bring me back to life so she could kick my ass."

The cops both laughed.

Shay threaded her fingers between James'. "Do the cops need any more statements from you?"

"Nope."

"Then let's get in your truck and go home."

James offered the deputies a polite nod and walked off toward his truck with Shay's hand in his.

"It's time to see who will become the Mud Kings," Royce announced.

The gathered bounty hunters and trainees cheered. James watched, his arms crossed as he leaned against a wall.

"First, everyone in the pit."

The men all marched into the pit.

"Take off your shirts and roll around like pigs."

The men blinked and stared at him.

Royce glared. "What, you too prissy to get dirty? I want you fucking muddy before you try to become the Mud Kings."

The bounty hunters and trainees yanked off their shirts and dropped into the pit, and soon everyone was coated with grime.

James chuckled and headed over to whip off his shirt and coat himself with mud. Even though he wouldn't be going for at least twenty minutes, he wanted the conditions to be as close as possible between him and the competitors. He left the pit and re-crossed his arms.

"Now, this is a team challenge as I explained before." He grabbed a box and walked toward the assembled rows of bounty hunters. He started handing out pink and neon yellow bandanas to different men.

Kevin eyed his pink bandana. "Uh, Staff Sergeant, why these colors?"

Royce shrugged. "Why the fuck not?"

He continued down the line and handed Lachlan a pink bandana. "You got a problem with this too, kid?"

Lachlan shook his head. "Nah, I just think about what Marcus Aurelius would say."

"And what would he say?"

"He'd tell me that pink used to be a man's color back in the day, and he'd tell me to grow a fucking pair. It's just a bandana. But fancier talk than that, and in Latin or some shit."

Everyone laughed, and Royce smiled, as did Trey and James.

"Good attitude, Lachlan."

"Whichever team wins will take on Mr. Brownstone," Royce announced.

Several of the men exchanged glances, but it was Max who spoke up.

"Just to be clear, he's a team by himself?"

"I don't need a team," James rumbled.

"That's right," Trey announced. "Because he's *James Motherfucking Brownstone*."

Everyone laughed.

A few minutes passed as Royce continued handing out bandanas. Among other men, Trey, Lachlan, and Kevin were on one team. Max, Shorty, Manuel, and Russell on the other.

Royce waited as the men filed into the pit. "Remember, the point isn't to kick people's asses. You just need to get at least their head past the ring line." He pointed.

A circular line surrounded the bulk of the large mud pit, leaving only about a yard of soft mud outside the perimeter, but it was enough space that a person could get shoved out without landing on the much harder cement.

"I'm gonna kick your ass out of this pit first thing, Lachlan," Shorty announced. "Then we can see what Marcus Aurelius says about that."

"Sun Tzu called and told me, 'Know yourself and know Shorty's mom. You might as well, since a hundred other men do.'"

The gathered men hooted and hollered.

James grinned. *Things have changed in such a short time, even for Lachlan. And now several of the men besides Trey have worked jobs. The agency will only grow from here. Fuck, this thing's actually working.*

Shorty grinned and gave Lachlan a nod. "All right. We'll see what's what in the pit, bitch."

"Lachlan," Trey called. "Come over here."

The nineteen-year-old headed over to his leader.

"You stay behind me, and I'll stay behind you. No one surprises our ass, and that way we can always survive. That's the whole point of this shit. The team."

Lachlan nodded. "All right."

Royce walked to the edge of the pit and raised his arm. "Teams ready." He dropped his arm. "Fight."

Several men charged each other. They grappled, struggling to gain purchase. Two men forced each other out only fifteen seconds in. More than a few got picked off because they focused straight ahead and weren't ready for a surprise attack from the rear.

James grunted his approval.

"Keep your situational awareness, men," Royce shouted.

Lachlan and Trey stayed back to back, pushing and prodding as yellow bandanas came after them.

Manuel tried to charge them from the side, but the pair grabbed him by his armpits and tossed him past the ring line.

A large group from the yellow bandanas charged Trey, thinking the morale victory would be worth it. They lost several men for their trouble.

Grunts and the slap of skin and splash of water and mud dominated the arena for the next several minutes until it was down to only three pink bandanas: Trey, Lachlan, and Kevin versus six yellow bandanas, including Shorty and Russell.

Shorty circled Trey and Lachlan with a grin on his face. "Come on, Lachlan. You gonna hide behind Trey all day?"

"I'm not fucking hiding behind Trey. I've got his six, bitch."

Royce and James watched from the sidelines in silent approval.

"Don't you want to settle this shit man-to-man, Lachlan?"

"Nah."

Shorty barked out a laugh. "You too chickenshit now just because I beat your ass before?"

"No, because I was thinking like a dumbass when I was a gangbanger, but Staff Sergeant and everyone has set me straight."

"How's that?"

"I should think of the team first, and my bitch-ass second." Lachlan sniffed. "Yo, Trey! I'm about to do just that. You feel me?"

Trey nodded. "Do what you need to do."

James narrowed his eyes, not sure what was happening, but Royce watched with a huge smile.

Shorty shook his head. "Don't get ahead of yourself, Lachlan."

The younger man burst from behind Trey, his heavy footsteps splashing mud everywhere. The yellow bandanas blinked in surprise, pivoting as a group to go for him and exposing their backs.

Trey and Kevin shot forward and slammed into the rear of the enemy team, shoving and throwing elbows. Three men were out of the ring before they even knew what hit them. Two others managed to turn, but Trey and Kevin bowled them over. One of them grabbed Kevin's ankle and took him down with him.

That left Trey and Lachlan versus Shorty.

"Let your plans be dark and impenetrable as night, and when you move, fall like a thunderbolt," Lachlan shouted.

Shorty grinned. "You ain't won yet, Sun Tzu."

"You want to take him on yourself?" Trey called.

"Nah. I ain't got nothing left to prove to no one but myself. Let's do this shit, Trey."

Shorty shook out his hands. "Bring it, bitches."

Trey and Lachlan charged Shorty and yelled at the top of their lungs. Lachlan threw his arms around the solid man's waist, and Trey slammed into his top. The smack of muscle meeting muscle echoed, and Shorty fell, his head landing outside of the ring line.

Shorty laughed. "Damn. Why you got to do me like that?"

Lachlan stood up and stretched out a hand. Shorty took it, and the other man helped him up.

"You all right, Lachlan."

"Same, Shorty."

"The pink bandanas are the Mud Kings," bellowed Royce. "Now rest for twenty minutes, and let's see if you can win against your boss."

James took several deep breaths. Defeating his men through brute strength would be trivial, but that wasn't the point. Trey and Lachlan eyed him with hunger, Kevin and some of the others with open fear.

The bounty hunter allowed himself a grin.

These are good guys, but Royce is right. It's time to remind them why this is the Brownstone Agency and not the Garfield Agency.

James backed up until he was right in front of the line and crooked a finger. "Bring it, if you've got the balls."

Kevin and three other men rushed forward screaming. James spun to the side, and their momentum carried them outside the pit.

"You've read what Sun Tzu has to say and Marcus Aurelius, and other generals and wise men," James shouted. "I'm not a fucking wise man. I'm just an asshole bounty hunter. I don't even have a college education."

The men cheered.

James charged two men near the edge. They crouched, ready to grapple, but he dropped into a sliding tackle that sent one man into the other and both past the line. James hopped to his feet, ready to face the remaining men.

"Winning isn't always about strength. It's about using your fucking head, making sure good people have your back, and sometimes just being damned lucky. You never know when a clown could save your ass."

Half the men cheered, the other half murmured amongst themselves in confusion.

A few easy pushes and takedowns followed, until again only Trey, Lachlan, and Kevin remained.

James pounded a fist against the hard planes of his mud-covered chest. "I could toss any of your asses halfway across this pit, but I won't, because I'm making a point."

Lachlan rushed forward trying to flank James. He didn't take the bait. Instead, he charged Trey and Kevin. The two split apart, but James grabbed them both by their shoulders and pushed them outside the line.

He spun and offered Lachlan a hungry grin.

The teen gritted his teeth. "Shit. It didn't work."

"I'm sure there's plenty in Sun Tzu about repeating yourself, but nice try, kid." James stalked forward, his arms out.

Lachlan's eyes darted back and forth for a few seconds before he sprinted toward James and threw himself into a tackle. James spun with the man and stopped, letting the momentum send the trainee flying outside of the ring. Lachlan landed with a grunt and splash.

"Nice try, but always remember—sometimes you're just gonna lose." James grinned, and Lachlan gave a playful shrug.

The gathered men walked over to slap him on the back.

"Nice try, Lachlan," several offered.

"And James Brownstone is the Mud King," Royce announced.

The men cheered.

Shay settled at a table at the Leanan Sídhe and looked at the cleared-out area in front of the bar. A thick crowd surrounded it, eagerness in their eyes.

"You sure about this, James?" Shay inquired.

James grunted. "I can handle this shit."

The Professor moved into the performance area, and several people whistled. Others cheered.

"As you know, today, we have a rare treat indeed." He

pointed at James. "Mr. James Brownstone himself is participating."

The crowd roared their approval. James shrugged.

"As a condition of his participation, there will be no audio or visual recording." A disappointed sigh swept the room. The Professor held up a box on the bar. "Which is why we've confiscated your phones. If anyone secretly records this you will be banned from this bar for the rest of your life, but let's get on with it. We have four participants today, including myself and Mr. Brownstone. May the filthiest bard win!"

James was the first to go, so he offered as his opening salvo the limerick the Professor had previously enjoyed.

"There once was a man they called Brock,
Who worked like a bitch 'round the clock,
A vacation he earned,
For the lessons he'd learned,
Like fucking your mom with his cock."

The silence of the tomb gripped the room after completion. The seconds ticked by until the crowd all but screamed in approval and laughter.

The Professor waited for them to calm themselves before stepping forward to offer his rebuttal.

"There was a young sailor named Bates,
Who went off to sea wearing skates,
But a fall on his cutlass,
Has rendered him nutless,
Poor fucker's now useless on dates."

The Professor shot a toothy grin at James. After a moment, he realized the Professor's cheeks didn't have a hint of red.

So you're taking this shit that seriously, Professor?

After the third round, only James and Smite-Williams remained.

The silent tension that filled the room between rounds was more appropriate for a chess match than a filthy limerick battle.

The Professor's fourth and final salvo left James reeling, if only because he hadn't realized the rhyming potential of Dolores.

The older man cracked his knuckles. "Dethrone the champ if you dare, lad."

James marched in front of the bar. Murmurs and whispered filled the crowd.

Shit. I've used the ones up I thought up before that were any good. Maybe I should have talked to Anna more.

James looked at Shay. She grinned back at him and winked.

The bounty hunter cleared his throat, and silence again swept the room.

"A beautiful woman named Shay,
Who was well used to getting her way,
Took a liking to James,
Her sweet spot he slayed,
And she couldn't walk straight the next day."

After the cheers died down, James' stomach knotted as the implications of what he'd just uttered settled in. He couldn't even bring himself to look her way.

Oh, fuck. What did I just do? Shay's gonna fucking kill me.

He scrubbed a hand over his face.

"The fine waitress is going around with the voting box again," the Professor announced. "We shall see if the champion reigns, or if there is a new Bard of Filth."

A few minutes passed as the waitress collected the voting slips, the bartender counted them, and another waitress recounted them.

"We have a winner," the bartender announced. "The new Bard of Filth is…"

Everyone held their breath.

"Our defending champion, Professor Smite-Williams."

The gathered crowd laughed and cheered, but James barely noticed. He slunk over to Shay's table, staring at his feet.

"Are you being that much of a sore loser, James?" Shay asked. "I didn't realize you were so into this shit."

"No, I just… I'm sorry."

"Look at me."

James lifted his head. Shay wasn't glaring or red-faced. Instead, she had a huge grin on her face.

"I've made a big impression on you," Shay commented. "At least, *part* of me has."

James groaned. "I'm never gonna hear the end of this, am I?"

She snickered. "Nope."

The Professor finished shaking hands and headed over to clap James on the back. "Close, lad, close. You did a good job, and I think you sort of get it now. Not completely, but close." He leaned in and cleared his throat. "And I still haven't had a chance to thank you for the job."

James blinked. "Huh? *Thank* me? I texted you that it blew up."

"Aye, it did."

"And you're okay with that?"

"I told you before, James. I wanted it out of circulation, but I didn't know how to do that without risking people's lives. If it blew up and helped you take down some right bastards, I don't see the problem." He laughed. "Next time you have someone with the power of Mount Doom coming after you, let me know."

James grunted. "I'll keep that in mind."

Shay stood and tugged on his hand. "Let's get out of here. The Professor needs to mix with his adoring crowds, and I want to see if you can put words into action."

"What are you talking about?"

She grinned. "It's time for a little slaying."

FINIS

Thank you for reading my *Author Notes* here in the back!

Here we are rocking book 07 in the *Unbelievable Mr. Brownstone* series and (fortunately) you guys and gals have provided amazing reviews and purchased this series enough for me to think "maybe we can go to *twelve* books here..." And so, I plan on it. If the series is still awesome at twelve, we *might* squeak out sixteen.

But that's probably it.

In two books, we will have the 'summer special' that will be Alison coming home, but first there is a thunder down under effort that confirms *boys will be boys.*

Even when they are men, and should probably know better.

I was speaking with Martha Carr yesterday while eating lunch at Fuzzy's Tacos (in Roanoke, Tx.) We were talking the beats (the bones of the stories) for the next School of Necessary Magic and a small part of Shay as I told her what got written in this story, and what's coming up next.

While we were supposed to be working on more beats, what we really did was have fun dreaming up a new series. That series will have to be one that waits though, as we have a few to wrap up before we can even conceive of creating new books. (Not that Martha would hesitate to start something new. She is the queen of 'there are *never* enough projects' and I dread to hear what she thinks when she finds out about *that* comment.)

Fortunately, she is going to be tied up this month with her work, her books, and selling one house and moving plus another personal item or two...

So...let's not mention that little comment to her, ok?

Running a publishing house is a lot of fun. It's work (often, sometimes it is hard to figure out where fun ends and work starts) but I enjoy the opportunity to publish books in an industry that has given me so much pleasure.

Brownstone is now a legacy that has, at least for the summer of 2018, held on to many top spots in the sales charts and I'll always smile when reading these books in the future (yes, I read my own books) knowing that we did it.

We made a bunch of fans super happy.

EAR CRUSH

If you like listening to stories, and want some that are NO WHERE else (including Tabitha's Vacation) check out a new podcast!

Ear Crush delivers professionally narrated science

fiction, urban fantasy and other great stories from best-selling authors like Michael Anderle (hey, that's me!) Craig Martelle, and others each week.

Join the email list to be notified of new audiobook releases and to be eligible for free stuff from LMBPN Publishing.

http://lmbpn.com/earcrush/

Ad aeternitatem,

Michael Anderle

- Rule of Magic (4) - Dealing in Magic (5) - Theft of Magic (6) -
Enemies of Magic (7) - Guardians of Magic (8)

The Soul Stone Mage Series

* Sarah Noffke and Martha Carr *

House of Enchanted (1) - The Dark Forest (2) - Mountain of
Truth (3) - Land of Terran (4) - New Egypt (5) - Lancothy (6) -
Virgo (7)

The Kacy Chronicles

* A.L. Knorr and Martha Carr *

Descendant (1) - Ascendant (2) - Combatant (3) - Transcendent
(4)

The Midwest Magic Chronicles

* Flint Maxwell and Martha Carr*

The Midwest Witch (1) - The Midwest Wanderer (2) - The
Midwest Whisperer (3) - The Midwest War (4)

The Fairhaven Chronicles

* with S.M. Boyce *

Glow (1) - Shimmer (2) - Ember (3) - Nightfall (4)

CONNECT WITH MICHAEL ANDERLE

Michael Anderle Social
 Website:
 http://kurtherianbooks.com/

Email List:
 http://kurtherianbooks.com/email-list/

Facebook Here:
 https://www.facebook.com/OriceranUniverse/
 https://www.facebook.com/TheKurtherianGambitBoo
ks/